Music for the Third Ear

Music for the Third Ear

A Novel

Susan Schwartz Senstad

PICADOR USA
NEW YORK

MUSIC FOR THE THIRD EAR. Copyright © 2000 by Susan Schwartz Senstad. All rights reserved. Printed in the United States of America. No part of this book may be used or reproduced in any manner whatsoever without written permission except in the case of brief quotations embodied in critical articles or reviews. For information, address Picador USA, 175 Fifth Avenue, New York, N.Y. 10010.

Picador® is a U.S. registered trademark and is used by St. Martin's Press under license from Pan Books Limited.

The following chapters have been published in the U.S. and Norway, some in adapted form and/or in translation into Norwegian: 'Zero': *Vinduet #1*, 50th year, Gyldendal Norsk Forlag, Oslo, 1996; 'Music for the Third Ear': *North Atlantic Review*, #8, Stony Brook, NY, 1996, and *Signaler* '97, J.W. Cappelen Forlag a.s., Oslo, 1997; 'Forensic Evidence': *Ragtime*, Flemasjonal Kulturforening, Oslo, April 1999; a merger of the two chapters entitled 'Theft' into one short story by that name: *North Atlantic Review*, #10, Stony Brook, NY, 1998; a 3-chapter novel excerpt, 'Zero', 'Seeds of Patriots and Heroes' and 'Ground Zero' with an introduction by Thomas E. Kennedy: *The Literary Review*, Fairleigh Dickinson University, Madison, New Jersey, USA, October 1999.

For help in researching this novel, the author gratefully acknowledges *Mass Rape: The War against Women in Bosnia-Herzegovina*, edited by Alexandra Stiglmayer, translation by Marion Faber, University of Nebraska Press, Lincoln and London, 1994. *Rape Warfare: The Hidden Genocide in Bosnia-Herzegovina and Croatia*, by Beverly Allen, University of Minnesota Press, Minneapolis, Minnesota, 1996.

ISBN 0-312-26621-9

First published in Great Britain by Doubleday, a division of Transworld Publishers, a division of The Random House Group Ltd

First Picador USA Edition: February 2001

10 9 8 7 6 5 4 3 2 1

For the children . . .

The novel is not the author's confession; it is an investigation of human life in the trap the world has become.

Milan Kundera
The Unbearable Lightness of Being

. . . If I could drive you out of your wretched mind, if I could tell you I would let you know.

R. D. Laing
The Politics of Experience

Part One

I
TOLERANCE

Music for the Third Ear

The mock old-fashioned door opened and there they were. But they didn't have long black coats and 1940s suitcases. This was now, not then. They had ski jackets and nylon zip bags, dark hair, yes, but not long noses or glasses. They were Mesud and Zheljka Nadarević, a Bosnian Muslim man and his Croatian Catholic wife. No Hungarian Jews here. She couldn't take any World War Two Jews under her protective, comforting wing and so would have to settle for Balkan refugees instead.

When she opened the door, Mette had her camera ready – loaded with black-and-white film. But the picture was all wrong. It didn't resemble the frayed-cornered, gray and yellow photograph she had of her own parents when they came out of the refugee camp. There they stood, outside the door of the Norwegian family taking them in during the optimistic adjustment period of the mid-1940s. That photograph is a post-war cliché: a thin young woman wearing a coat several sizes too large clings close to the shoulder of a tiny young man. He smiles with his mouth, but his eyes are as dull as death. She seems cornered. The baby in her arms looks like laundry.

Whenever Mette asked her parents to tell their story, they had fed her the same canned speech: wonderful Norwegians had offered them a room. It cost nothing and included food. Then her father found a job in another Jew's shoe store and a fifth-floor walk-up flat in central Oslo, near the synagogue. The outhouse was in the courtyard.

She felt like a mother bird each time she saw that photograph, wanting nothing more than to spread full her wingspan, as if to shield some hole in history. Those same wings trembled now, ready to enfold and soothe the traumatized couple to whom she so generously offered refuge.

But the picture wasn't right. For one thing, upon seeing the camera, the man put his hand up to cover the lens, like a father defending his family not necessarily because he was close to them but because he was the master, let there be no mistake. With his other hand he shoved his wife behind him. When Mette had the film developed, that photograph showed only blurry, flashbulb-whitened fingers from behind which there glared one focused, furious eye.

It was all wrong.

Of course, when Mette had asked her husband, Hans Olav, a fatherly man older than she, for permission to respond to the call for temporary housing for refugees broadcast by *TV2 Helping You*, she had

14

hoped he'd say no. Even if Mette had married a gentile (she had guiltily described him to a friend as 'Aryan-tall-and-handsome'), some part of her didn't really want to take in these poor, fleeing victims – a Muslim and a Christian who worshipped Mohammed and Christ and thus were trained to hate the Jews.

She wanted to think of herself as a good person. Truly. History had come around to her land again, at last, and now was her chance to prove she wasn't so selfish, egotistical, cowardly, despite having been spared all that her parents had suffered. She felt a rush of warm self-loving tears, felt her insides melt. 'Yes,' she said. 'We have rooms to spare in this big house with no children.'

After the flash, the young, bony woman who emerged from behind her compact, stern husband did not look like Mette's mother at all. Where the one had been frail and cowering, this other one seemed about to explode out of her skin, as if there were too much horror for that abraded, papery shell to contain. How could a mother bird wrap sheltering wings around such a body? They'd be hurled back, broken off, in some arched-back protest against embrace.

'*Snakker dere norsk?*' Obviously not. 'English, then? Do you speak English?'

'I do. Quite well.' It was the woman, Zheljka, who spoke, while the man, Mesud, just glared.

'Well. Welcome to our home.'

15

*   *   *

Mette showed them the guest suite – a spruce-paneled sitting room which led to a bedroom and bath done in peaches-and-cream – the kitchen, and the cellar laundry facilities. But not the living room. This had been a source of conflict between Mette and Hans Olav. It wasn't that he was against her offering to take in a refugee family; he understood Mette's need to help, felt she had a greater capacity for empathy than he, though she had some tendency toward self-sacrifice. But he valued his *husfred* – 'house-peace' – the fact that after work there was an undisturbed place where he could lie back in his deep brown, glove-leather easy-chair, sipping his Hennessy and listening to his music, a place where the premises had been set long ago and were not negotiable. The living room was decidedly not available for communal use: he considered that a rather modest demand.

Hans Olav didn't mind having a victimized woman sheltered in his home. But that husband might be trouble. What had he done during the war? Murdered? Tortured? Had he raped other men's wives while they were raping his? Would Mette be safe while Hans Olav was at work?

Nor was he reassured when he arrived home that first night. 'What are they like?'

Mette hugged him, suspiciously long. 'Just wonderful,' she began. 'They're so very nice, and grateful to be here.'

16

After fifteen years of childless marriage, Hans Olav knew that Mette had a double line of communication, which he compared to music: what she said was often lyrical, decorated with treble flourishes, baroque grace notes and trills; what she meant, however, had a bass line in a minor key, more like a requiem. When Mette twittered, 'Just wonderful,' her song told him, *It's all wrong*.

'Let me meet them.'

Upstairs, the host couple stood outside the guest suite's closed door, Mette wedged behind her husband's shoulder, as if taking refuge. Hans Olav's hand was raised to knock on the door when he heard, coming from within the room, words of a language he did not know but which had a music he could interpret. Hans Olav heard modulated, male anger. It sounded as if the woman inside were being scolded and was crying softly, perhaps pleading. Sensing a potential for violence in the man's voice, Hans Olav knocked hard: three solid raps with his knuckle. This was, after all, his house.

The door opened startlingly fast, leaving Mette cornered and Hans Olav with a hospitable smile muscled abruptly onto his face. Mesud stood before them breathing hard as Hans Olav towered over him. The two men challenged each other with their eyes to see who would look down first; as neither yielded, a border was created in that doorway, guarded on both sides.

Hans Olav reached out his empty right hand

and spoke, insisting on his own language, '*Hallo og velkommen.*'

Mesud, still not looking down, called out, 'Zheljka!', who came to the door and, with a tired face, accepted Mette's invitation to eat dinner with them.

Mette loved to cook, loved food, ate well as evidenced by her abundant hips and large thighs which she found unfashionable, perhaps even ugly. Actually, she had no other choice but to eat. She was God's miracle of survival incarnate, conceived and born in the liberators' hungry camp, growing, through some capricious, even perverse, holy intervention, fat and juicy within the starved body of her mother. Mette's mother would point to the false teeth she was fitted with once safely in the arms of the rescuer nation, Norway, and say, 'My teeth you ate, *Mama zisa*, so you could live and be born. I would have given you all of them – and my bones, and my blood . . .'

They named her Mette, a play on words from their new language that was also their prayer for her: when people have had enough to eat they say, *Vi er mette*, we are full, we are not hungry any more.

As a teenager, each time Mette tried to diet, her mother would stare in tear-filled horror at her half-filled plate. '*Mammele*, like a bird, you eat. I could count all your bones with one eye. Haven't Jews starved enough yet?' But it was her father's glaring silence which exerted the real power: Mette had to eat, got good at eating.

And her parents' eyes were always on her. Even after they died.

Tremulously hovering over the refugees at the dinner table, Mette filled their plates, salted their food, and asked Zheljka, in English, 'Do you need any warm clothes? Long underwear makes a big difference in this climate. I've got extra.'

Before Zheljka could respond, Mesud asked her something, probably for a translation. She answered him, and he said something back to which she seemed to object. He spoke again, firmly, and only then did Zheljka answer, looking at Mesud in between her words, 'We have got everything we need.'

Mette flinched, as if slapped. Then Zheljka added, 'Thank you, very much.'

Mette tried again: 'Mr Kaldstad, my husband, Hans Olav. He drives to Oslo every morning. If you need a ride, you can go with him.'

Zheljka translated, Mesud spoke to her, she answered him, he said something longer. Then she addressed her hosts, sounding somewhat apologetic, yet perhaps belligerent, or proud: 'We were given bus passes, maps, instructions, addresses . . .' She shortened what he had said, as if censoring. Again she added, 'Thank you, very much.'

Mesud ate rapidly, silently, looking at his plate. His face was heavily marked; some of the scars looked old, like acne, while others appeared fresher,

19

like wounds. His was a face which seemed to have been attacked, whether from within or without.

After a long silence, Hans Olav addressed Zheljka: 'Tell your husband that my company is hiring. What is he trained to do? What did he do at home?'

When Zheljka had translated this question for him, Mesud glared searingly into Hans Olav's eyes across the table. He paused for a long moment and the two men seemed to hold their breath. Then he spat out four words which Zheljka, eyes averted, translated one by one: 'Is.' 'This.' 'An.' 'Interrogation?' Mesud continued to hold the other man's eyes, and then, as if to assert his undisputed victory, looked down at his plate, filled his fork, and brought it to his mouth.

'Please, my husband does not mean to be rude,' Zheljka said. 'We come from war. Can you understand?'

Mette's wings flew open. Now, *this* was right; *here* was something she could do. Her eyes softened, she got a sweet music in her throat and warbled, 'Mesud,' to get his attention, then again, 'Mesud,' to soothe, and once again, 'Mesud,' because his name felt so good in her mouth.

The man looked up and answered her songful, teary eyes by dropping his fork from the level of his mouth down onto his plate, scraping his chair back, then abandoning the room. The sound of that scraping chair reminded Hans Olav of something, but he couldn't place what.

Zheljka folded her napkin carefully next to her

plate as she rose, then pushed in her chair. 'Pardon me. Thank you, very much.' She followed her husband upstairs.

That night, as they lay in bed, Mette said, 'I'm so glad we've done this,' which Hans Olav understood as, *Help me, I'm afraid.*

'Your parents would be proud of you.' He put his large hand on her head and was not the least bit surprised that she began to weep, muffling her sobs in the hollow of his embrace. He stroked her hair softly from the crown of her head to her neck, over and over, careful not to make a sound.

In her dream that night, Mette was a tiny chick, newly hatched, featherless and wet. In the nest with her were two large, round birds, a male and a female, with overstuffed chests like magpies. Her job was to fly, however awkwardly, to the water's muddy edge, dredge up and swallow tiny stinging eels, and then fly back up to feed the two large birds. They rammed ravenously angry, open beaks down her tiny throat, brutally pecking out nourishment she had no choice but to provide.

Hans Olav was not much of a dreamer. This particular night, however, he dreamed he heard splintered music somewhere in his house, the pressure in his ears varying as the bass rhythm was hacked into sporadic lengths. As if sneaking up on an enemy, Hans Olav tiptoed, as lightly as a large man could, toward his own most comfortable living room easy-chair. There, to his great irritation, sat Mesud.

The music got louder then. Hans Olav thought at first it was Norway's national anthem, but no, it was Mahler's Fourth Symphony, his own personal favorite, the one constructed of fragments which come together rather than themes which are taken apart, the third movement during which he always pictured a horse slowly pulling a rustic hearse as bittersweet, nostalgic folk melodies alternated with tones of tender grief.

Mesud sat, head in his hands, elbows on his knees, hunched over. Slowly he looked up. In Mesud's eyes, Hans Olav glimpsed a shattered mirror of atrocities, witnessed or survived, which he was mortified, on the other man's behalf, to have seen.

The following days began the delicate process of establishing rituals for sharing living space. Unfortunately, the food Zheljka bought, probably with money from social services, more than filled the shelf Mette had allocated in the refrigerator. So Mette cleared out a second shelf, squeezing her own relishes and jams in with the meats, finding an old Christmas marmalade Hans Olav's sister had made and which she, in her ambivalence about Christmas, as well as about her sister-in-law and oranges, had forgotten ever to serve. She glanced up at the menorah hanging unused on the kitchen wall; clinging to years of accumulated kitchen grease was a layer of dust.

They decided to divide up the cooking hours, Mette insisting on holding the pattern she and her husband were used to: eating at 6 p.m., clearing the table together, she finishing the dishes in time for them to watch the TV news at 7 p.m. So Zheljka would cook first.

In practice, however, Hans Olav came home not just to the smell of cigarette smoke, but to a stench of onions and garlic he found distasteful, to unswept breadcrumbs on the floor under his dining room table; these people used bread for everything and at every meal. And to half-prepared food: Mette had not wanted to disturb their guests' dinner with the noise of her own cooking and so had waited for them to finish before she began. Hans Olav had to choose between eating fast, which he hated, or missing the news, which he felt was a betrayal of his duty as a citizen of a country so small that all its inhabitants must consider themselves accountable for the actions of the State.

The first phone call for the refugees came after the couple had been with the Kaldstads a week, interrupting one of Mette's and Hans Olav's dinners. The male caller wanted Mesud. Hans Olav answered it in the living room. He could have told Mesud to use the cordless phone, or one of the more privately situated extensions. Instead, he held the receiver in his hand and called out for him to come there. After all, the man spoke a foreign language; no one could actually eavesdrop.

But Hans Olav considered himself an expert at listening to the music under words. What he interpreted went like this: first came tones asking questions. Then stern, military-like commands were shouted softly, were bitten into small, muffled portions through a clamped jaw as if in controlled anger. After that drummed three or even four insistent, mock-calm repetitions of what sounded like the same message. Finally, as if compliance had been achieved, the conversation ended with a flat closure. When Mesud hung up and disappeared upstairs, Hans Olav told himself, *This man's a leader in the Resistance.*

One evening, some two weeks after the refugees had arrived, and after both couples' dinners, the Kaldstads' doorbell rang. When Mette answered, there stood a youngish, round woman in a headscarf next to a hard-bellied man who carried the kind of burgundy-colored plastic bag that only the State-run wine and liquor monopoly stores use. The man nodded and said, 'Mesud?'

Mette smiled too broadly. 'Please, this way.'

A few minutes later, the doorbell rang again. One rather frail man seemed to study the door-sill while another craggy fellow, who reminded Mette of a defeated militia man, said softly, 'Mesud?' Mette showed them both upstairs.

Hans Olav, somewhat irritated, answered the doorbell when it rang again. He let in a husky man in his mid-thirties who carried not only that same distinctive red plastic bag but also a guitar case. 'I thought Muslims didn't drink,' Hans Olav said to Mette, as he returned to the TV room and closed the door.

Mette and Hans Olav could hear the laughter, the music, the raucous singing, the scuffling upstairs. Were they dancing? Wrestling? Even turning the TV louder didn't drown out the party going on in their house. Mette walked out into the quiet downstairs hall, looked up toward the light shining through the curtained glass of the guest room door, then returned to the TV room. She closed the door and put her index fingers in her ears.

Even after it was late, Hans Olav's and Mette's house was full of strangers. The music had become quieter, perhaps morose. Voices could be heard, sounding sometimes deep and serious, and at other times agitated – even angry.

On his way to bed, Hans Olav found himself outside the refugees' door, preparing to knock. At first, he knocked too softly to be heard, then he knocked harder and, when the door finally opened, looked in. He didn't recognize the room: it was as if the door had opened onto another country. Or was it another time?

All the men sat in a rough circle smoking cigarettes and hunching forward to look at some papers together. A couple of them were on the floor, knees drawn up, eyes moist – from the smoke? From drink? Or tears? One was singing a slow song.

Through the door into the inner room, Hans Olav could see the shapes of the two women lying on the bed, clothed and apparently asleep. This was a meeting of the Resistance, he was sure.

Ever since he was a child, a seven-year-old in 1940 at the start of the German occupation of Norway, he'd known about the Resistance, about the paper-clips people wore on their collars as a secret symbol of revolt, about the red caps everyone put on to signal solidarity until the frustrated Germans, ludicrously, made the wearing of red woollen caps illegal. The Germans also forbade them to sing the Norwegian national anthem.

Suddenly, looking into that group of men, Hans Olav remembered an event from that time. On December 19th, 1943, a fully loaded German munitions ship exploded in the icy Oslo harbor shattering most of the glass in their neighborhood, even exploding their apartment's window frames right out of the brick walls. No one in Hans Olav's family was injured. The explosion, as it turned out, was simply an accident, not even an act of sabotage, but until they found out just what had happened they hid, terrified, in their cellar bomb shelter convinced that a full Allied invasion had begun.

And Hans Olav remembered how, with no glass available, they had nailed boards over the icy, gaping window holes in time for the relatives to gather there for Christmas dinner. They were all at the table about to take their first bite of the festive food they'd smuggled in from a countryside farm when big, sturdy Uncle Reidar, his father's older brother, slowly stood up. The noise of his chair scraping along the floor as he rose caused the whole group to look up; seeing Reidar on his feet, they put down their forks and grew silent. Then Uncle Reidar began to sing, in a strong, dark baritone, the banned anthem, an act for which their quisling neighbors might well have had him jailed. Hearing the song of their occupied country, whose first line is, *Yes, we love this land*, Hans Olav's father, his brave, balanced, rational protector, began to cry! His father. A man. Crying!

The ten-year-old boy felt his throat thicken, first in the swollen rush of all his own choked-off weeping, but then in shame and anger. Little Hans Olav clenched the muscles in his chest, his throat, clamped his jaw, and took a vow within a freezing corner of his heart: he would never, ever cry again.

Now, over fifty dry-eyed years later, he stood outside the door of these, he assumed, Resistance fighters, whose song might just as well have been their anthem, and felt, for the first time in all those decades, his own tears – for his father's pain, for the losses of occupied lands everywhere, for the wounds of war. He stood in the doorway yearning, more than he could bear to know, to be invited in.

Instead, he had to find some excuse for having knocked. He searched his mind and found something worthy of the memory of his father's customary tact. 'We'll be going to bed now,' he said tenderly. 'Please lock the front door after your guests have gone.'

One of the men translated for Mesud who, looking up, nodded seriously, politely – perhaps even warmly. But once that was done, he resumed his conversation with the others. Hans Olav felt like some sergeant who had interrupted the general with a relatively insignificant detail and had been courteously dismissed. Or like a ten-year-old.

He closed the door a little harder than he'd intended and went to bed. But not to sleep. He told himself he was listening for whether these drinking Muslims would head for his liquor cabinet. All he could hear, though, was how very contained the sounds in the room next door remained.

The next morning, Zheljka came to Mette with a request. 'I wonder, Mrs Kaldstad, is it possible I use that room near the living room now and then?'

She meant Mette's study. There, not having to accommodate to anyone's taste but her own, Mette had created for herself a robin's-egg-blue haven, a virginal nest of ruffles and flounces. Here she sewed, wrote letters, read. Her books were in this room, the ones she didn't want strange eyes perusing, the ones about infertility, or the Holocaust.

Mette did not dare ask Zheljka why she wanted the room, nor assert anything about privacy or the limits to hospitality. Instead, she said, smiling, 'Why certainly,' then added, 'Whenever you like.' Somewhere inside Mette, though, a crow cawed and flew a little higher in her chest.

The doorbell began ringing during the day while both Mesud and Hans Olav were gone. One woman came at a time and Zheljka would lead each of them into Mette's study and close the door.

Mette took her reading, or her knitting, into the living room when one of these visitors came, occupying the chair closest to her study door in order to listen to the noises leaking from the room. She told herself she ought to go cook something, or visit a friend, but somehow she couldn't leave those sounds.

Some conversations were quiet throughout. Distant. But most often they only began that way: calm, tentative, whispered. Then came the sound of the visitor half-choking. Zheljka's voice soothed insistently and with authority; she repeated the same sounds, almost like a chant, or an exorcism, until the other woman's voice began to quaver and then, at one pitch or another, with one volume or another, to cry out, break down, sob.

Slowly, then, the weeping would abate and the room become silent, as if empty. Then both women spoke again, softly now, more loosely. Once or twice at these times, a small laugh would even trickle through the walls.

Eventually, the door would open and Zheljka would show the exhausted woman out. Zheljka looked somber and contained during these exit scenes, but as soon as the front door closed she would lean her weight against it, her eyes closed. With trembling fingers, she'd comb her hair back from her hairline again and again, like a hard caress, as she breathed in small, diminishing gasps. She'd turn then and head quickly for her rooms upstairs.

But soon the bell would ring again.

At first, this emotional music bleeding through the walls only made Mette curious; she coolly analyzed the sounds, naming one *pain*, another *anger*, without, however, feeling anything herself. But after several days of listening, the sounds began to etch themselves into her. Then, in the midst of one such session, there came a particularly raw and horrified cry from within her room.

That cry was merciless. It rumbled and quaked in the body; a tectonic groan too huge for any mouth to hold, it tore instead right through the chest, ripping through the flesh in protest, a cry of 'NO!' as furious as it was fruitless.

That sound hurled Mette back to a night she'd been careful never to remember; she'd even made sure to forget having forgotten it:

She was five years old, back in her childhood bed, awakening to a light that seeped in through her half-opened bedroom door. She must have been sleeping with one arm stretched out over the side of the bed, for there, curled up on the floor, lay Mette's mother, huddling under the child's tiny arm, pressing her nose and mouth against Mette's skin as if frantic to fill her lungs with her daughter's scent and being. The woman choked off gasps of weeping, rocking herself back and forth and chanting, *Mama zisa, Mama schena,* as if Mette, even in her sleep, should mother her own mother.

But it was from out beyond her weeping mother that howling sound came, in through the cracked-open door. Out there, Mette saw her father crouched on the sofa pounding his blue-numbered arm against the upholstered back, and heard him gag repeatedly on that impotent word, 'NO!' He spat out curses, in Yiddish, in Hungarian, in a polyglot of anguish and fury Mette's ears could not hold. Mother and father together in grotesque counterpoint, *Mama zisa, Mama schena,* on top of 'NO! NO! NO!' wove a futile fugue, one voice desperate for comfort, the other simply desperate.

Lying there, pretending to sleep, Mette could give those people nothing, could ask for nothing. She could only try to be feather-light, invisible, that her existence might not burden them, might add nothing to their pain.

Now, in her own living room, grown-up Mette knew that these were the sounds which had been with her always, the sounds with which she had shared a womb. She ached, torn by contradictory desires – to embrace that dead moment and make it her own, or to cram it back into the grave of silence. Either way, however unwillingly, she now could not but remember.

In tears, Mette approached her study door

and knocked. The door opened a crack, Zheljka obstructing her view deeper in, where, it seemed, a woman held her breath.

'Yes?'

Nothing.

'Nothing.' She was outside her own door. 'I'm sorry. I'm so sorry – for disturbing you. I'm so very, very sorry.'

That night, as Hans Olav came in through their front door, Mette said nothing. But he asked her, 'What's up?'

Mette stood without speaking, her face tear-dirtied, her eyes flitting to the banister, to the paintings on the wall, to the floor. And then she blurted it out, entreating: 'Please, Hans Olav, send these people away. Please make them go.'

'Mette, I'm surprised at you. No. Of course we can't send them away, they've been displaced enough, poor souls. And why would you want to do that? You of all people?'

'All these years married to me,' Mette shrieked, 'and you still don't understand, do you? You don't understand a thing!' She turned, fled to her study and shut herself in.

As soon as he finished his dinner that night, Hans Olav went up to the refugees' door and knocked. Zheljka opened. Mesud, Hans Olav saw, was folding clothes neatly, placing each piece in a nylon zipper bag.

'I'd like to invite the two of you down to our living room to have a drink with us.'

Zheljka translated. Mesud looked up and replied with several short sentences which Zheljka answered, in a tone that sounded pleading. He said one more sharp word, after which she addressed Hans Olav quietly, 'Thank you, very much, but no. We are packing.'

'What? Are you leaving us? But where will you go?'

'We move out tomorrow, to friends of ours.'

Mette stood by the front door the following morning managing not to cry as the couple left. She had the camera hidden in her pocket. Not willing to risk meeting Mesud's stop-sign hand again, Mette waited to take a picture until their backs were turned, until they were walking out the door, down the steps, leaving her house forever. The resulting snapshot showed the frame of a mock old-fashioned Norwegian carved door surrounding the blurred, moving backs of two anonymous ski jackets.

That evening, Mette and Hans Olav ate their dinner at 6 p.m. precisely. After the news, Hans Olav played, over and over, Mahler's Fourth Symphony, the fourth and final movement now, where the soprano sings, *'Kein Musik ist ja nicht auf Erden/Die uns'rer verglichen kann werden.'* 'There is no music on earth/That can compare with ours.' He listened, sitting in his easy-chair in the living room, his head resting back, a tear sliding softly down his cheek.

Mette, meanwhile, sat closed in her study. She slumped there, mute and wingless, listening deafly to the walls.

Zero

*No light reaches that clutching void. He cannot
ascertain, compare, protest that there where he
should swim he can only curl, clamped in a womb
that wishes him dead. He cannot know what ought to
be.*

*But Zheljka knows. And cannot unknow that
jellyboned growth like some cancer, her – she retches
up the word – her – oh God must have had something
else in mind when creating such a thing, her – please,
die! – son. If only the germ which made him had
drowned in the sack it came from. But no: seed-
sharks without number had been cockvomited into
her by who knows how many gloating, vicious, so-
called* normal *men, in an abandoned grade school
classroom shouting, 'I'll fuck your mother, make
me hard!' That guy from the café, remember? Who
said he wouldn't, got hit and then he did. And
the neighbor, Drago, the one with that big dog,
remember? He's* Komandant *now; he slimed her ass
and cunt. And mouth. (No meal ever again without
that taste of them, no word. Ever.) And others, baying*

their patriotic glorysongs, jackal-packs of them, every day, every day if not from twelve o'clock to one, from three to four, Zheljka and thirty other not-dying women taking turns dribbling rotting semen into one waterbucket toilet, stinking.

He cannot know that through the membrane boundary between him and she who contains him, there where blood should feed, there seeps also bitter venom. Nor that she ought not pound with bloodless fists against that muscle she holds clenched to strangle him, having failed to scrape him out with her nails, her needles, her scathing potions, trying instead to pound him lifeless from the outside in, to crush his softboned, newbrained skull. All he knows of life is the venom and this huddling, bobbing in the wombstorm. It is just how it is and always has been, and would be, all Time.

So when, inside her, music is not there, not one lullaby, and when no one strokes his skincage house and no one rocks or pats or croons, he does not know to miss it. (What thousandth millennium desert lizard dies of longing for the sea?) He just retreats to his bellymouth and imbibes the dregs her body involuntarily serves. He grows little for his starving, but gradually, nonetheless, despite her (she thinks it is to spite her), grows large enough to push against the walls with arms as if to dig a bigger hole. Not like a miner digs, or a gravedigger digs, or a pit bull digs, but like an arm in a nightmare sweat that would push back the wall caving in upon it, crushing its bone and being.

36

And for every inside-toward-outside punch of his arms or legs or head or rump she answers with her own self-bruising fist; he kicks her and she punches him back, hurting her much more than him. He punches her, though not her, for she is only some of all he could not know – just there. To her, however, it is she whom he has punched and so she punches him as if he were all his fathers and as if she could torment them, every single man, by ravaging the issue of what they forced inside her, spurted inside her.

To her, he is all of them: the oozing pimply young one in the battering queue who covered up his eyes yet exposed his groin. And the tall one with tarantula hair crawling out from his too-tight buttoned collar while he unzipped. Or that fat one, the last she saw on that particular day, who threw his coat across her face, shouting, how could he be expected to get hard with those two ugly fisheyes goggling up at him.

Yes. Punch until it bleeds, until he dies, until he gets a taste of what his fathers did.

Then one day she is emptied of him in rhythmic spasms she cannot hinder. Pulses convulse him down her skullcrusher tunnel, which she struggles to shut even as it opens, squashing his skullplates to a dull clubpoint, making of his head a ram for bashing his way out.

There glows a first-ever point of light. But when the clenched bone tunnel holds him fast and the belly-mouth tube is crimped and the poisonfood can hardly trickle through, metal claws pierce into the tunnel.

37

Cold and bruising against his scalp, these yank at his head, uncurling him, lengthening him, prising him outward – where he is met by Zheljka's next attempt at murder, now with the weapon of her thighs. She tries to smash his head between those two great skin slabs until someone grabs her knees and pries them wide apart, and then he must struggle against her hands, her clawnails, sharp things pulling at his hair and going for his eyes. These, too, they throw aside. They will not let her kill him.

Instead, while flailing without purpose at the insubstantial air, his bellymouth is cut, the icy atmosphere initiates his nostrils and he unthroats the cry that comes before all words. The child is born, stunned alive. Punches of light jab colors at his eyes, the red of blood, the yellow of walls. The black of Zheljka's glare.

Those hands of hers still reach to claw and punch and so they take him from her. To a house on dry land, a dry aquarium where he rests, awash in cries of others, otherwise conceived. There he lies.

She will not have him.

Nonetheless, someone picks him up, flannel-wrapped, tense and tiny as a universe before the bang, and holds him over her to see what she will do.

Her arms lie dead. She faces anywhere but there.

'Take him.'

'Take him away!'

'Take him. He needs to nurse.'

'Let the shitbag starve.' But now she only whispers.

*   *   *

Slowly, then, despite herself, Zheljka's pale exhausted hands take toward themselves the violation that is him.

Now her fingers do not try to rip, or choke. Nor do her arms clutch to kill or maim. Instead, they bend beneath him, as if cradling. He looks at her, sees black again, the only color he has always known, there in her two wide, wet, shining pupils. She holds him, crying.

'God, are you listening?' Her face is moving closer. 'God, I ask you . . .' She is breathing in his odor, her lips are on his forehead. 'Who ever will care about this . . .' She holds him up and sees him, 'Horrible child?' Tiny eyes milk giant eyes, sucking in, undeciphered, her love and kill-love meanings.

He gapes. Even as a squall of hunger rises, as his stretched-flat tongue quivers, pink and tiny, and as he lets loose with the very shriek of all that came before, the mother cannot close her ears. She thinks she hears him beg, and can only yield. She thinks she hears him command and, cowed, obeys. And thus, resigned – though in no way reconciled – she lets his rape-fathered facemouth ravish her breast.

Her son.

She names him, Zero.

II

LOVE

Seed of Patriots and Heroes

Zero is four, small for his age. He stands in the street before dusk – an ancient cobblestone Roman street too narrow for cars, wide enough for motor scooters, too bumpy for bikes. At dinnertime on a Sunday summer evening, the world rests. A radio is playing from a third-story window. From a second-floor kitchen in a building at the back of their little alley someone fries food and yells to someone far away in some other room. But not to Zero.

He holds a cap pistol in one hand. His arms dangle at his sides, his thin legs planted like a movie cowboy in a shoot-out scene as he listens for his mother calling him in to eat. He's hungry. Their apartment faces the alley, one flight up. The railing in front of their window looks squashed, as if a balcony had been crushed almost flush against the wall, leaving only room for some plants. His mother keeps a pot there of blotchy, drooping flowers which need more light than the alley can provide, and more water than she gives. She has the window by the railing open even though, on such a warm day, sour waves of garbage stink rise up into their living room from the cans below. Still, a breeze, however scented, might blow in as the day cools down.

Zero knows nothing about the plant living or dying and nothing about the garbage smell; it's just the sight and smell of his life and nothing more. But he knows he's on the street alone.

Then the man who owns the vegetable store just across the street appears. He unlocks the metal wall that store-owners roll down over their windows at closing time. He raises it, like an armored window shade, but only halfway up. It clangs and echoes. He looks over at Zero, nods, then ducks down under the wall and enters his store. Zero smells the deep-dug humus odor wafting coolly from within the open hole. The man ducks back out carrying a bottle of olive oil, noisily pulls down his robber-shield, snaps the heavy padlock in place and is off down the street again.

Zero is hungry and no one calls to him. He has also run out of caps. He takes his pistol up and pretends that around the corner leading from his alley to the somewhat wider street is an enemy, the wily Giant, who knows Zero is back there. Zero pushes his back against the building's stone and slides slowly along it, stepping silently, his pistol pointing heavenward right in front of his nose, waiting for the instant of his sneak attack. When he's sidled far enough, he peeks around the sharp, chipped-masonry edge of the building at the bad guy Giant whom he's sure to have caught unaware.

But Zero jumps in startled confusion at what he sees: just down the crooked street, standing in front of another armored wall where, on weekdays, they sell only wine, where old men sit all day playing cards on rickety tables whose skinny metal legs tilt and shift, grinding against the uneven cobblestones, there stands his mother! When had she left home?

She stands talking to a stranger woman and man. At first he thinks it's that Mesud man who just started visiting, and every time he comes his mother whispers and Zero gets sent to the *portiere*. But no. This other strange man and a strange woman are holding hands and wearing nice Sunday clothes while his mother leans her bony shoulder against the metal wall, her head lowered, her hand in front of her face. Zero knows she is crying; she's been crying all the time lately. He wants to run to her, but of course he knows he mustn't: at home, when he tries to pat her shoulder as she sits crying, she flinches out from under his touch and snarls into her hand a muffled, 'No. No more, Zero,' she says. 'It's enough now.'

So he just stands there with his shoulder sucking the day's stored heat out of the masonry wall. Small corners of the half-torn political posters, which some people slap up during the day and other people rip down at night, layer upon angry layer, tickle his arm as he slowly begins to take aim. The little boy lowers his pistol in an arc, like the second hand of a clock progressing from twelve on its slow way straight out to three. The one eye he keeps open, to get a better shot, has placed the faraway head directly behind the sight sticking up from the tip of the barrel of his gun. First the head of his own mother, but then, changing his mind, of the strange man standing near her.

He has the enemy right where he wants him. 'I'll kill you, you man,' the dialogue runs in Zero's mind. 'I'm Zero the Kid. I'm going to shoot you DEAD!'

But he doesn't shoot. Yet.

His gun is still aimed but he listens and looks. The man puts his arm across his woman's shoulder, leans toward Zero's mother and Zero can almost hear his word-splinters, pointy and sharp: '. . . Your husband said you'd *agreed* . . .' and '. . . best for the *boy* . . .'

Suddenly the man shouts, *'You have to tell him!'*

Zero fires!

'POW! POW!' The capless pistol clicks, once, twice, and the boy starts running away. Away from the grown-ups, down the cobbled street expecting to be chased, waiting to hear his mother shout his name, demand angrily, 'Get over here this instant, Zero, you hear me?' But no sound follows him and he stops his running, looks back.

The couple is walking away, heading for a big brown car, the strange man's arm still across the strange woman's shoulder. His mother hasn't moved, still leans against the metal wall, face in her hands. Slowly she turns back toward their alley without looking up to see him.

Should he call out? He decides not to. And just

when he's decided that, he hears his mouth yell, 'Mama!' And then he's running toward her, his mouth shouting, 'Mama!' and still she isn't looking.

When he reaches her, he flings himself around her bony hips. But she throws her arms up into the air, as if he'd pointed his gun at her.

'No more, Zero,' she snaps and twists her hips out of his grasp. She jams her key into the street-level lock, opens the heavy door and then lets it slam behind her.

He is alone in the alley again, his pistol hand hanging at his side.

Zero is in his pajamas, the ones with the little brown cowboys riding horses up and down his arms and legs, chasing horned cattle and half-naked tiny Indian men with tomahawks and scary feathers. He's under the covers and the nightlight is on because he screams if it's not and he should have been asleep long ago but he isn't.

When his mother tiptoes in, he pretends he's sleeping but watches her from behind the edge of his light summer blanket. He sees her go to the wooden armoire, which has a closet on one side and drawers on the other, inside of which his clothes are kept and on top of which his mother stores the things they rarely use. She gently places his little stool in front of the armoire then stands on it, stretching high up and just managing, with fingers like claws, to tap the suitcase that's always up there.

Every night, that suitcase's handle casts a shadow

way up on the wall that looks to Zero like the Giant's angry eye glaring down at him. Now, as his mother rocks the suitcase closer to the edge, the eye stretches bigger, tilting, blinking, lifting up from the wall and then spreading out, growing vast and nasty across the ceiling. Zero almost screams, but then, as his mother gets the suitcase in her hand and steps down off the stool, the Giant's eye that was always there – is gone.

The suitcase must have been dusty because when she puts it down, she wipes her hands on her pants and her sleeve across her face. Or is she drying tears? She opens the suitcase on the floor, opens the armoire doors and drawers and starts to take his clothes out, folding each piece neatly and placing it in the hard-sided suitcase.

He wants to pretend some more that he is sleeping but hears his own drowsy voice stir the night-time air: 'Mama? What are you doing?'

She jumps, startled when he speaks. 'Shhh, Zero. Go to sleep.'

He can hear now that she's crying. He doesn't know what to do. 'Mama,' he says again, 'where are we going?'

'Zero, please. Just sleep.' Her voice is wet and faraway. One second she is standing over there by the foot of his bed in front of the armoire folding and folding. And then, suddenly, she's here beside him, on the edge of his bed, grabs his little body up in her arms, blankets and all, and holds him to her, sobbing, rocking.

He doesn't know what to do. He struggles to get his arms out of the embrace so he can put them around her neck, his little hands patting her shoulders rhythmically. Then they're both crying.

'No more, no more, no more . . .' is all she says, and she kisses his eyelids, his forehead, his cheeks.

He hears his own voice cracking, 'But where are we *going*, Mama?'

Instead of answering him, she hurls him down, abruptly, on his bed, then stoops to straighten the covers carefully, tucking in the blankets as if swaddling an infant, all the time weeping and saying nothing at all. She leaves the suitcase where it is, partially packed, steps out of his room and shuts the door.

The Giant, missing from the empty ceiling now, is surely on the loose. Zero reaches into the heap of clothes beside his bed and finds his pistol. He slides his hand and the gun carefully under the pillow, his finger on the trigger.

They Die Anyway

You must have your own ideas about it, Beate, must have heard about it on the news. But the strange thing for me is that, while they were – doing that to me, to us, systematically, strategically, day after day, in that grade school building, our neighbors . . . The strange thing is, how come the walls didn't bleed? Or scream? Or why was the sky still blue?

And how come I can still remember when Mesud and I met and fell in love, how I played with the swirl of black hair around his navel, or the thinning hairs around his high forehead, how I traced the lines left from his acne and made up stories about islands and lakes and highways, as if the scars were a treasure map and his wounds were the clue to some hidden fortune?

What were you doing those days, Beate, way up here in Norway, in frozen peace?

I was lying with him in Sarajevo on a blue afternoon like today, one of those spring days when the open windows let in a slightly chilly square of air which the sun heats to radiance, one of those days when you can't tell the difference between sunlight and birdsong, the birds sing light and the sun shines music . . .

But wait, you don't know anything. I guess this was in April since we met during the winter semester. I'll start even earlier: I'd been at the Sarajevo Music Conservatory just a little more than half a year studying piano and Mesud and I met at a bar where his friends played in a little rock-and-roll band after work. We out-of-town girls were the favorite prey at that place. We had nobody at home waiting up for us so we could stay late at parties, smoking hash, strutting around in our fancy jeans and imported shoes, and our perfumes that had designer names.

When Mesud came up to our table, I was with my girlfriends from school, I couldn't understand a word he said with that Bosnian accent of his and his lousy grammar. I'm Croatian, remember – our language waltzes, his plods. So I kept making him repeat himself, and then I'd poke my friends with my elbow and wink, which of course ticked him off. I made fun of him for everything, like how he worked in a print shop without ever reading any of the books he printed, mass producing knowledge without getting any smarter.

That came back to haunt him, by the way. Later he discovered that the very shop he worked in had turned out some of the worst Ethnic Cleansing propaganda, the stuff the Serbs used against his people. But that was later . . .

No matter how I teased him, Mesud kept coming back, even finding the café in the park where we all congregated after school, drinking dark coffee and crafting giggly commentaries about every fellow who passed by. I invented songs to typify how each guy walked and accompanied myself on a cardboard practice-keyboard my father had brought back for me from one of his trips. I had it lying on my lap. When Mesud walked up – oh, how bold I was – I looked him in the eye provocatively, and grandly pounded massive, complicated chords on my paper piano. But he just kept on coming.

Most of his friends, the guys in the band, had these young wives they left at home while they went out to parties and to bars. I must have visited him a dozen times at home – he had this huge Muslim family – before I'd believe him that he really wasn't married. I say Muslim, but not the kind with veils or anything, and Mesud drinks and eats pork, even during Ramadan. His mother fussed over me there, feeding me meat stews with apricots, and honey cakes for dessert. She is – rather, she *was* – even shorter than I am but really round, and kept complaining I was too skinny because I came from the coast where we ate too much fish and not enough meat.

I was nineteen, he was thirty. It took two whole months before I'd sleep with him.

I rented a room with another Conservatory girl also from Dubrovnik, in the center of Sarajevo – at Marin Dvor, which may sound fancy but actually the building was pretty run down – and there was just one double bed which Sandra and I shared. One day Mesud found a trail of little blood droplets on our sheets. You should have seen him. He grabbed my arm, and when he didn't find anything (I'm scared of needles) he got hold of Sandra's arm. She had tracks. That's when he announced that he was marrying me: no way he was going to have me getting into drugs, he said.

But all that was later, closer to summer. The day I'm talking about was a gorgeous spring day, like today. But of course, there spring is warm.

This was after we'd started sleeping together. My roommate had gone home to Dubrovnik for the weekend and I was lying in Mesud's arms, on his left, no, it was his right shoulder, making a slow whirlwind in the spiral of hair around his navel as he told me stories about taking all his brothers and sisters to Mount Igman, one of the forests outside Sarajevo, long before any sniping started. Mesud's the eldest and his father died when he was only thirteen so he did a lot of fatherly things with his younger brothers, hunting, exploring.

The room had one of those deep-set windows that opens like a French door, only not all the way down to the floor, just down to a broad window sill and there were silky, white, floor-length, see-through curtains hanging inside the blood-red, shantung drapes we drew closed only at night. I often sat on that window sill, my back to the frame on one side of the window and my feet propped up against the other side. My parents had shipped me my piano, the little Petrof *pianino*, but still I liked sitting by the window with my cardboard keyboard on my lap, indulging in silent arpeggios, and lurid glissandos, improvising chord progressions with soaring variations on themes of my own invention. God, I was dramatic.

But that day, the one I'm talking about, I was in bed with Mesud, him naked and me still in my slip, a peach-colored satin slip. We had drawn the white silk drapes and they were blowing and I was stroking Mesud's belly around and around in rhythm to the undulating curtains while he crooned on about childhood escapades on Mount Igman, about stealing honey from bees, building forts from branches, skinning rabbits with pocket knives.

Then, all of a sudden, a bird was in the room! A bird had flown right in through the open window and was slamming into the high ceiling again and again, looking for the sky. She was little and black, with a sheen of violet and a tapered, double-pointed tail. A swallow, you know, one of those birds that coasts high up all day, their wings hardly ever flapping, coming down to earth only at sunset when thousands and thousands of them dive together and settle into nests under the eaves of the old villas, filling the spring and summer dusk with their small, wild calls.

God knows what made that little bird so disoriented, what separated her from her flock, making her fly so low during the daytime. Maybe she'd

been sucked down by the wind. Captured. I don't
know.

What I do know though is the look of Mesud's
naked body, stretching, reaching for that swallow
each place she tried to rest – Mesud up on tiptoe,
one muscular arm extended for maximum reach, his
fingers dancing to grab the bird as she perched
to catch her panicked breath on top of the dark
wooden curtain pole, her chirping's rhythm dis-
rupted, disturbed. I can still see that tiny bird's
chest, her rapid breathing and Mesud's man-chest
filling up, to stretch his reach as long as possible. I
have this vision of the luscious flexing in one of
his buttocks, the strong ridge of muscle climbing his
back, as the billowing white curtain slides itself
like fingertips with each new breeze ever so lightly
across his torso.

Then the bird took flight again, flapping
frantically from one side of the room to the other,
though swallows would far rather glide. Mesud kept
on chasing after her. She crashed into the ceiling
and dropped panting, stunned, but rose again,
taking momentary refuge on the carved-wood flower
trim atop the massive bookcase – a mock-antique,
heavy, dried up and dark. Mesud stood now in the
center of the room, hands on his hips, chin raised,
staring up at her, out of breath. My young, near-
virgin eyes saw nothing but his sex, his strength, his
dark, grown-up man's beauty. The bird, she had
other concerns, but not I.

Flapping wildly again, now in the right direction –

toward the window – she was caught up in the fist of that white, blowing curtain, became confused, and Mesud finally got her.

He brought her to me.

I remember how his thick fingers, with those hairy knuckles and those nails inked permanently black, wrapped themselves around that fragile, silent, beating, blinking bird. He held her before me and I wondered at such man-hands around a tiny being, and that he could bear the pounding warmth of her fluttering against his palm.

That contradiction, that's what I loved – man-ness. Nothing at all like the effete boys my parents wanted for me who never used anything but their wit, boys so like myself I couldn't bear their presumption of authority over me and every other girl. Mesud was a force of nature. Plant his tree-root feet in good soil and they'd sprout a gnarly trunk even a hurricane couldn't topple. With such a man, I believed, I could submit, quit struggling, be taken.

What I'm asking you, Beate, is this: how it is possible for these memories to live inside this same head with the memories of what came after? I won't describe those horrors, just picture the worst violation you can imagine, but make it your own crotch spread out there, gaping, dripping.

I know you don't need me to describe the details, Beate. Death has its own language.

But can you tell me this: how can those memories live side by side with the other ones? Why doesn't my brain split in two like an axed apple? I almost wish it would because that's what may make me insane, you know. I picture Mesud naked that sunny April day with the tiny bird in his fist, a fist capable of crushing her, and I want to shriek at the God who disappeared, *How is this one body of mine supposed to hold those two times?*

Some of the other women here do it differently. They won't know any more that what came before really happened. They've wiped it out so nothing was ever anything but horror. I wish I could do that, you know, because I wonder sometimes which memory hurts me worst. Not which is the worst memory – I'm not crazy, for some strange reason. But now, when I dream about the good times, it's a nightmare.

That day in the sun I started calling Mesud by his childhood nickname, *Medo*. It means 'little bear'. He lies beside me at night again now, but I cannot call him *Medo*. He says to me, *Zheljka, this is me, Mesud, your Medo. I'm not those others*. I have to tell him though, *Yes. You're one of them. Your kind did this to us*. He gets so angry then, he punches the mattress next to me so he won't hit me.

I know I'm not being fair. I guess. He tells me the war destroyed him too, *raped his soul,* he says. It seems everybody wants to be the victim. I just keep silent. I don't point to the burn scar on his palm from the barrel of a machine gun – not a machine gun pointed at him, but one he was holding.

I don't mention Zero.

*   *   *

I saw Mesud naked yesterday afternoon, in the sunshine in our room. For a moment my heart almost remembered fluttering. And I looked at the damage they'd done to the beautifully swirling black hair around his navel. I looked at all those scars and I tried to see them like a map, like the scars on his face, a new treasure map. And then I almost said, *Yes, my Medo, it* is *like you're one of us.* But I refuse to give him that.

It's good to talk to you this way, Beate. People walking by must think I'm strange sitting here speaking to a tombstone, but then, these Norwegians think all immigrants are crazy anyway. Or else they assume whatever way we do something is just the way it's done back where we came from. So now they'll think that all Croatians sit and talk out loud to graves, like it's a tribal rite, a Balkan death ritual.

Even you might wonder why I picked out your plain gray stone to talk to. Maybe because *Beate* is one Norwegian name I recognize, from Mary in the Mass. And your headstone says you weren't much older when you died than I am now. Just last year. That seems funny – there wasn't a war here at all, but still you died.

Maybe, too, I picked you because no one puts flowers on your grave. And, now that I think about it, there's that little bird carved right by your name.

Which reminds me. I forgot to tell you what

59

Mesud did with the swallow when he caught her. He pulled the curtains aside and loosed her into the air. And if you could simply take that for granted, then you don't know how lucky you are. It doesn't matter though. I'm sure she's dead now, anyway.

Ground Zero

Not once, not twice, but three times Mesud failed to bring himself to enter the ancient Roman alley, via del Pozzuolo. Finally, straightening his sagging tweed jacket, a donation from CARITAS, the Catholic welfare committee which had succeeded in tracing Zheljka's whereabouts, Mesud managed to turn into the sunless cul-de-sac and stop in front of number eight. They'd told him Immigration had placed her here after the camps – alone, he presumed – and that she now awaited his arrival. When he saw 'Nadarević', his own last name, next to the lowest of the doorbells, he flinched.

Whatever has happened, I'll forgive her. I forgive her everything, he rehearsed.

He looked at the hairs on the back of his thick, nicotine-stained fingers as he rang the bell. Working hands. Man hands. No one can guess where hands have been, what hands have done, or can they? A tinny intercom voice, in foreign Italian, asked, 'Who is there?', an absurd question, so unanswerably complex he almost laughed.

Simplifying matters, he said, in Serbo-Croatian, 'It's me, Zheljka – Mesud.'

'One flight up.'

As he entered Zheljka's building, something sharp stuck into the sole of Mesud's shoe, a toy tin soldier, its weapon now crushed flat into its chest. He slipped it into his pocket, wondering at his return to a world where small boys and their playthings still existed.

In the hallway, he thought of that crazed bird that got trapped in Zheljka's room in Sarajevo, early, at the beginning, how it had crashed its head again and again against the high white ceiling. Mesud had caught the bird and set her free. *Big strong man.*

He went on. First, there were five steps to a landing, as many steps as the years they'd been apart. Then the stairway took a turn to the right, but as he assumed she'd be standing above with the door open he paused at the landing. Looking up through the bars of the railing, he saw her scuffed navy-blue high heels, like the fancy ones she'd worn when they'd gone dancing in some other philosophy of life. That was before he'd been forced into Bosnia's government army, back when he was a rough-lived man of thirty, coarse enough to make the wild cravings of a well-raised nineteen-year-old seem tame in comparison. When both he and she believed he could keep her safe.

By the next step, when Mesud could see how her dark-blue skirt hung over bony hips, and before he could reject the images, visions came of the humiliations his enemies probably had perpetrated against him there on the terrain of his wife's slim body. He'd heard the rumor going around that, soon after he'd left, Zheljka had been dragged from the bus she was trying to escape Sarajevo on and held prisoner by Serbian soldiers. *Sullied* was one word he wanted not to think. *Whore* was another.

I forgive her.

Rising another step, Mesud saw Zheljka's white blouse and the tired, respectable ruffles decorating those small breasts, the breasts he'd thought of every single day, struggling to preserve a memory of them as unbitten, unslashed, his young wife's breasts.

Then Mesud saw Zheljka's face. Those elegant, angular, Slavic features of five years ago looked now as if they'd been exploded and put back together slightly wrong – like Zheljka, but less so: askew, sallow, sunken, bereft. He thought her face frozen, until he noticed her chin trembling, her eyes blinking rapidly, how she kept on swallowing. The tears that came to his own eyes then were more than he'd thought himself capable of.

He had planned to keep it simple, simply to say, 'Hello, Zheljka,' to give them time, to take it slowly, for once to keep his furies underground. He struggled for control, but in order to speak he had to unclench his teeth, and once his jaws had opened Mesud lost control. He clutched at Zheljka's body, aching to fill his lungs with her, fill his mouth with her, fill her up. He wanted to come home.

Zheljka jumped back from his touch with a gasp. Was there to be no safe harbor for him anywhere? She tried to slam the door on him but he had come too far.

'Zheljka. Please. Let me in.' He held his hands in the air as if she had him at gunpoint. 'I won't touch you, I promise.' She backed away from the door.

Zheljka had only learned the day before that he was even alive. Not dead, her dead Mesud. In fact, arriving. How would she manage?

She occupied the wooden chair and motioned for him to take the sofa. That way, his back was both to her narrow bed, with the crocheted coverlet she'd arranged so the frayed patches lay hidden along the wall, and to the upright piano she'd wangled out of her landlord. She kept the keyboard closed and draped across it a violet-embroidered scarf with a ragged, bright orange fringe that she'd bought at a Roman street market from Russian immigrants selling all that they possessed. From the vantage point of the sofa, Mesud would also be less likely to eye the door to the other room of the apartment.

Zheljka had placed her stained teapot on a white doily in the absolute center of the rickety coffee table. The white mug with the painted flowers climbing its handle was all right, but that second cup . . . On that one, a cowboy swung a rope. She wished she owned more cups.

Even seated, Mesud filled her room, this missing husband whom once she believed could keep her safe. He was here now in this very room. And unchanged, but for those fresh wounds amidst the scars from adolescent acne, scars whose pattern she used to trace, either teasingly, calling him 'Your horror' (her father was a judge), or while kissing them one by one, as a mother kisses a sore. His eyebrows still sprouted recklessly, and that compact body still pulsed as if struggling to contain impossible contradictions. That once had aroused her.

So, they sat.

Reaching in his pocket for a cigarette, Mesud found the crushed tin soldier he'd picked up outside her door. He placed it, teetering, on the table between them. Zheljka's eyes were caught by the movement, but she forced them to look elsewhere, at her hands in her lap, her interlaced fingers, at her thumbs as they traced the lines on her palms. Mesud, meanwhile, looked back and forth from his hands to his heavy boots. The only sounds came from outside – some man across the alley arguing with another man farther up the street, some mother calling out of a window for 'Giuseppe . . . Giuseppino.'

'Mesud,' Zheljka began.

His name was in her mouth again. Had she kept it on her tongue, like one of her communion wafers, those first months after she was taken, when they must have come for her again and again, as he knew they'd done with the captive women? Had she refused to speak it when they'd demanded the name of the coward who'd abandoned her to his enemy, hoping to taunt her with it as they took her? *I would have saved you if I could*, he would have shouted, but he and his name had arrived too late. 'Well, Zheljka, you're looking fine,' he said instead, quietly.

'Oh?' she asked, then paused. 'Have you been in Rome long?'

He stood and began to pace the room slowly. 'Couple of weeks. I'm out near Eur. There's a group of us they're trying to place. But – they assume I'm moving in here. With you.' Her body stiffened and her eyebrows raised.

His pacing quickened and he picked up first one object and then another. From the shelf over the tiny sink in the kitchen alcove he took a spoon with a clown's face on it. He looked at it and put it down. From the bureau across the room he picked up a pink plastic hairbrush and ran his palm over the bristles, pulling out a nest of Zheljka's glossless dark hair. On the coffee table, the broken toy soldier wobbled. Zheljka didn't speak.

'They haven't given me work yet,' he continued. 'My Italian stinks, though I don't have to read books to print them, as you remember, so I don't know what they're waiting for. Did you hear me, Zheljka? They assume I'm moving in here. With my wife. A person might make such an assumption, no?'

'Where have you been?' Even Zheljka heard the accusation in her tone.

Mesud stopped his pacing and turned on her.

'Why, on vacation, didn't you know? Holiday at the seaside.'

'Don't, Mesud.'

'You want to know where I've been? What I did? Huh?' He leaned over her now, half whispering, his face so close to hers she felt the heat and she sweated. 'You want to know how I killed people in the war? Or, when they captured me, what kind of prisoner I was, dirt in my teeth? Or which way I headed when they finished with us and dumped us across the lines like garbage? Which part of my story do you want to hear, Zheljka?'

She gripped the sides of her chair. 'I can't, Mesud. I'm sorry. I can't.'

Zheljka sighed when he moved away from her to resume his pacing, hands in his pockets.

'So what do we talk about? Maybe the family.' Mesud stopped in front of the piano. Throwing aside the velvet shawl, he opened the keyboard lid and struck one disconnected note after another with a rigid index finger, in rhythm to his words: 'My. Mother. Is. Dead.' He banged down a clump of keys, black and white. 'Shot in the head in the living room while Senada watched, her own daughter. A neighbor I grew up with bragged about it, laughing, in the prison camp one day while he was beating me. And how is your family?' He hit some treble keys and spoke in sing-song: 'Are your parents dead too?'

Zheljka didn't answer.

Mesud sat down then at the end of the sofa nearest her chair and let his forehead rest on his palms long enough for his breath to slow. When he spoke, his eyes sought hers.

'How *are* your parents, Zheljka? Really. Are they still alive?' He pictured how she'd wept in the tiny Sarajevo apartment they got when they married, homesick for the brightly polished stone streets of Dubrovnik's Old Town, and for her parents, who refused to speak to her as long as she was with *that primitive brute,* and had not even attended their wedding.

'Mother is alive,' Zheljka said, eyes averted. 'About my father, we know nothing. He left to fight, just after you did. Mother waits by the door for him.'

'Were you waiting for me, Zheljka?'

She shut her eyes.

'I'm sorry,' he said. 'That wasn't fair. Tell me about you, Zheljka. What do you do? Are you working?'

She paused, looking once again at the stroking of her thumbs. 'No. I'm not.'

'How do you live, then? Who pays you?'

'The State pays refugees for a while.'

'But only till they find us jobs – or manage to export us.' His eyes squinted, his head cocked to one side. 'They told me you've been here a long time, what have you been doing? Where do you get money?'

She was about to cry. He demanded information and she refused.

'What are you, a hooker or something?' He was standing, shouting. 'Is that why I can't come home?

Is this a whorehouse, with my name on the door-bell?'

'Mesud hush! I have neighbors, the window is open!' And of course she was no whore, she protested, and of course he knew that.

And he did, too. He'd imagined this reunion a thousand times, and here he was fucking it up, him and his bloody temper. What did she want? he asked her. Did she want him to leave? Widow her twice?

'Just tell me what to do. If you want me to I'll go.' He straightened the ragged lapels of his jacket and headed for the front door, as if he meant to leave. He held onto the knob so tightly he saw his fingers turn white, just like the hands of a soldier from his group who'd drowned clinging for dear life to the pylon of a pier – except his head was one meter *under* the water: the would-be rescuers couldn't pry his panicking fingers loose to pull him to the surface until it was too late.

Mesud might even have left, but the top button of Zheljka's blouse had come undone; he glimpsed his wife's flesh and did not go. Instead, Mesud walked the three paces it took to cross the room to where she sat, hardly breathing. It was a long journey. On the way, he imagined slapping her, how his palm would tingle from the touch of her soft skin. Then he pictured grabbing her body against him, whether she could bear it or not.

What Mesud actually did surprised even him. With his left hand he lifted her chin and with his right he began lifting his shirt. It was a polo shirt, not tucked in, easy to lift. But he slid it up slowly, his fingers clutching its border as he raised the hem and exposed first the swirl of dark hair around his navel, which she would surely have recognized but seemed to have forgotten. Then he began uncovering tens of circles of fused, inflamed flesh in some emerging order, a plethora of small scars, not randomly placed, not accidental. Circular scars about the size of the singeing end of a burning cigarette, and straight scars the shape of a glowing pliers' mouth, scars in a pattern slowly making sense as he raised the curtain of his shirt: a word of tortured flesh glowed there on his chest, purple and red. The word was: 'SERBIA.'

Her face was level with his wounds; she could have pressed her mouth to them, could have placed her burning cheek against his marked chest and breathed the once beloved odor of her man. But she didn't. Zheljka sat still and closed her eyelids slowly, escaping as she'd learned to do when they came for her again and again. She departed into vacancy and vacuum, shriveling somewhere closer to her core, where her being whirred like a disengaged gear. Zheljka left. All but her body was gone.

Mesud leaned over his wife, his arms tense and bulging as if burdened. Still holding her chin with one hand and now her forehead with the other, he forced a kiss onto her lips, forced his tongue between them as if to reclaim her mouth. She made no effort to resist, her tears soundless.

Only after that did Mesud notice the other door in the apartment, there beside the piano. He opened it. With his back to Zheljka, Mesud gazed long into the perpetual dusk of that other room, whose only window faced a wall. What he saw besides a wooden wardrobe was a little chair and a little bed. The blanket, which was too large, draped along the floor and something odd stuck out from under it. Mesud knelt, lifted the itchy wool and peered under the bed. He slid out a wooden vegetable crate holding assorted toys, building blocks, airplanes, and soldiers, many of them broken. The object which had caught his eye he now saw was a toy gun. A small rifle, a plastic semi-automatic.

Mesud carried it out, holding it by the barrel like a rat by the tail. He held it in front of Zheljka's face.

'What is this? Why is this here? Is there a child in this house? Do you have a child?'

'Yes, I do. A boy. His name is Zero.'

'Zero? That's not a name.'

For the first time since he had returned to her, Zheljka looked directly into her husband's eyes. She said nothing. Then, 'It is *his* name.'

'How old is this *Zero*?'

'If you're asking if he's yours, no, Mesud, he's not. I was not pregnant when you left me.'

'It's called *conscription*, Zheljka. I was fighting age. I had no choice!'

'Zero is four, Mesud. And there's only one thing in this life I'm absolutely sure of any more and that's that he isn't yours.'

71

Mesud dropped the weapon onto Zheljka's lap and turned his back. 'Where is he now?'

'With the *portiere*, at her cousin's in La Spezzia. For the week. She watches him for me sometimes. I wasn't planning on telling you about him at all.'

Several moments passed before Mesud turned again to his wife. He looked at Zheljka and she looked at him. 'Just one thing, Zheljka. Is he a Serb?'

'God Himself does not know which of them all the father is. Neither does Allah.'

The man seated himself, heavily, on the sofa. Mesud took the broken toy soldier from the coffee table and crushed it into a deformed clump of warm, malleable tin. After a minute, he lifted the teapot, filled the cowboy cup with tepid tea and passed it to Zheljka. Then he reached his hand across the table and said, only, 'Come here.' Moving as if her body were very old, Zheljka left her chair and sat beside him.

I forgive her, he vowed. *I forgive her everything.*

Well past dark, Zheljka offered Mesud Zero's empty room, but he slept on the sofa that first night. And the second night as well. By the third night, she allowed him into her bed, though not into her body.

As his hands and mouth moved to seek the very flesh he remembered, Mesud did battle with his imagination – of soldiers' mouths, soldiers' leavings, soldiers' diseases. But just that simple approach, just his male form hovering above her, sufficed to evince from Zheljka a reflexive scream, as if it all were about to begin again.

Still, somehow, and for the first time since all choice was denied her, Zheljka did allow a man, her own husband, gently, to lie beside her. She lay stiff and unmoving that third night and even the fourth. Then, on the fifth night, not yet weeping, Zheljka touched lightly each and every scar in the word burned into Mesud's chest.

As they lay there, wound by wound, on her narrow bed, Mesud whispered in his wife's ear, most simply:

'You know, I won't have any part of that bastard, their *son*.'

III
LOSS

Promise

Mette's father phoned one day, three months after her mother died of cancer, and told her to come.

He sat in the kitchen. At noon at their northern latitude, the light indoors ought to have been bright, even in mid-October, but filtered through the scratched window glass of the Stein apartment all daylight resembled dusk. It didn't help the atmosphere any that the kitchen floor was sticky, that the precious copper pots were encrusted with burned food, or that the square pine table Mette's mother had kept scrubbed to bony whiteness now bore tens of circular burns of the size made by hot coffee mugs.

Mr Stein was not sitting in his own chair, the one with the sky view through the hazy little window over the sink. He sat, instead, in his dead wife's place, back to the window, and to the hot-water tap which dripped at unpredictable intervals.

'Papa, it's disgusting here. You have to let me come and clean.'

'Sit down and listen.'

It wasn't often her father initiated a conversation with her. Mette sat dutifully, in her own chair, the one she'd grown up sitting in, though with her father at her right now, where her mother ought to have been. Not only had the family maintained assigned seating throughout the years, but the square table had even been kept at exactly the same rotation. Thus Mette was always faced with the table edge where, at the age of six, she had discovered how knives can cut. From then on, she was confronted at each meal with her petty destructiveness, those bird-tracks she'd carved so deeply into the wood that years of merciless scrubbing with a hard brush and green pine soap had failed to eradicate them.

'There are no Jews left for you in this country,' her father began, as if addressing the crow's-feet around her thirty-one-year-old eyes. 'All the boys at the Temple, they're married already.'

'Pa, don't start on me about marriage again. If there's no one here, I'll go to Florida, I'll go to Israel . . .'

He waved his hand as if brushing away flies. 'Don't talk. Listen. I want you to make me a promise.' He looked away, down to his hands clasped now before him on his wife's table edge. 'You saw your mama dying, now you believe people don't live for ever. So I want you to make me a promise? Like you make to someone on his deathbed.'

Mette would have said something about his good health, but he had told her not to speak.

'What matters most, I ask myself. You know what I think about marrying *goyim*. But any baby born to a Jewish woman is a Jewish baby, the ancient fathers, praised be their names, they knew a thing or two. So, listen: I didn't raise you in five thousand years of tradition to have the chain break here. Marry whoever you like, but promise me this – with a *sheggetz*, a *schwartze*, a hunchback, a beer-guzzling truck driver, anybody you want, God-forbid even a German – promise me this: you will have three children. Have four children, five children, ten, as many as you have time for, you're not young any more. *But not one child less than three.* Say, "Papa, I promise." Say it.'

'What are you talking about? Why?'

'Why?' He counted by uncurling his fingers, thumb first. 'One new Jew replaces your mother, may she rest in peace. Two, and you fill my place but the number of Jews in the world doesn't change, it stays just the same and they've won – we're fewer. You need three or more: one for her. One for me. And one for the six million we have to get back. Your mother only had you. You have to do better. Say it to me. Out loud, with your mouth: say, "Papa, I promise." ' He put the hand of his blue-numbered arm across the back of her hands, which were covering up her table-carving traces. 'Make me happy. Give me *nachas*, for once.'

Mette slid out from under his touch. Behind his back, she turned on the dripping tap, rinsed out a sour dishrag and began sweeping crumbs from the

79

counter. When she lifted the lid of her mother's flour canister to wipe away a clod of orange marmalade, small moths flew out. Her father's words arrested her on her way to entomb the bugs in the trash can beside the refrigerator. His voice shaped the same word twice.

'Promise!' he said, first as a booming command. And then, in a tone she didn't remember having heard from him before, he said it again.

'Promise,' he said, but this time it was a plea.

'How can I? Maybe no one wants to marry me. You want me to walk the streets just to make more Jews?' She had never talked so fresh to her father. Mette ran scalding tap water onto the dishcloth, then wrung it dry. The water stung the eczema sores on her hand. She should have worn rubber gloves.

'Figure it out. You're a smart girl. Just promise.'

Mette laughed, without smiling. 'Sure, Pa. I promise. I'll make at least three new Jews.' As she approached the table, dishcloth in hand, she saw that her father's cheeks were wet, his eyes averted.

His voice broke: 'Now, my sweet child, *kleine mädel* – stop trying to replace your mother and go home.'

When Mette phoned him later that evening to say that, like it or not, she was coming over to clean up, there was no answer. Nor when she rang again the following morning. She let herself into the apartment at noon, again at six in the evening, and then again at ten, but there was no one there. Nor was he there the next day. When she couldn't find her father the next day either, Mette phoned the Temple Community Center. Nobody there had seen him. She phoned the shoe store where he worked, his friends, even called some of their kids, people her own age from the synagogue whom she'd last seen at her mother's funeral, and who had asked her over and over what she was doing and where she was living and if she was married and then just nodded at her answers. But no one had seen him or heard from him.

Nor by the following day, or the day after that.

When five days had passed, the director of the Community Center called in the police to investigate a missing person.

Not until a January thaw did Mr Stein's body surface in Bogstadvannet. The police assumed he'd been out hiking and had a swimming accident. But Mette knew. Her father didn't hike, hated water, couldn't swim.

Mette had them wrap what was left of him in his white prayer shawl with the long white fringe. They buried him next to his wife.

Three years later, Mette married her boss Hans Olav Kaldstad, a gentile.

Theft

Nervous as a teenager preparing for a date, Mette tried on a beige polyester blouse with tabs she tied in a droopy bow. No. Wrong. Her hips looked like pontoons. How about hiding them under a paisley vest, and the eczema sores on her arms under a long-sleeved turtleneck? But then, why did it matter what she wore? She was heading for the *Asylmottak*, the refugee center, with a bag of clothes she and Hans Olav didn't want. No lady bountiful routine drove her to put on eyeliner twice, the second time because the first was too thick; it was Zheljka. She'd be there, maybe. And Mette wanted to win her back. *Back?* She'd never had her to lose.

Suddenly Mette yearned to take a nap, to lie – no, to flop – down on her bed atop the various rejected outfits and forget the whole burdensome confrontation. She'd been putting it off for days, had cleaner closets than in years, had even taken the kitchen cupboard handles off for the first time ever, scraping away small stuck-on crumbs that had insinuated themselves around the screws and caused no grief but now simply had to go. All the while, the big, black plastic garbage bag blocked the front door, evidence of her cowardice and intolerance, a judgment as indelible as the blue numbers tattooed on her father's arm. She couldn't make it right. Why try?

Mette looked in the long mirror over the bathroom sinks, above the white marbled Formica counter where her make-up was lined up, waiting, and smiled an opening greeting. *Hello, Zheljka. How good to see you.* But it wouldn't be.

How galling to chase after the young woman again, as if she had some obligation to her. Mette had housed them, charitably, Zheljka and Mesud. She and Hans Olav owed them nothing; they'd arrived as strangers and were stranger still by the time they left. Yet Mette felt somehow in their debt now that she'd given of her hospitality and warmth to those unknown, *unknowable* Balkan war refugees.

She resisted the call of her bed, the excuse of the cold Norwegian spring rain, of waiting for the sun to shine before she'd leave the house. Mette dressed herself and, her ribcage protesting, lugged the big black bag out the door leading to the carport.

A converted grade school, one of those utilitarian one-floor boxy affairs – room after room, and alongside them all a long hall – served now as the refugee center. The Serbs, Mette had heard, imprisoned women in such abandoned school buildings while raping them, and she wondered about Zheljka.

The room nearest the parking lot had been turned into a used-clothing store. There, refugees sifted through donations, sorting which to bundle up and sell by the kilo to a scrap recycler, and which to mend, iron, tag and display. Each item was priced according to the worth refugees might place on them, and there was no accounting for taste.

Much to their surprise, the refugee women found their store frequented by local suburban matrons who came in one at a time, obliquely, as if trying to be invisible. Each of their purchases was accompanied by some disclaimer, how they'd been shopping and shopping for something just like this, and couldn't find it *anywhere*. The resale shop's economic success surpassed all initial projections.

The air Mette gave off when she entered, opening and closing her umbrella forcefully the way a duck shakes itself upon coming out of the water, was of someone intimidated, or perhaps shy. She smiled too broadly.

'These are things my husband and I don't use,' Mette said to the only person there, a gum-chewing, dark-haired girl seated at a school desk trying on some of the donated jewelry. 'It's not that they aren't any good any more,' Mette explained as she unpacked the trash bag onto another desk, 'but I've put on some weight. And so has my husband. So you see, they might even be things we've hardly ever used . . .'

Without responding, the teenager took off dangly

brass earrings and put on a black polka-dotted pair, plus a matching headband which reminded Mette of a hairdresser from the fifties. This girl may not even understand Norwegian, Mette thought, and probably didn't care a fig what clothes Mette donated since none of them would fit her anyway.

'You can look at these later, I guess, or whoever it is who does that?' Mette said, complaining inwardly about being so ungratefully received.

A response finally came, in heavily accented Norwegian teenage slang. 'Not vaguest idea. Whatever.'

These people weren't going to make this easy, Mette thought, so she puffed her chest full of resolve, and asked, 'Is Zheljka here, by any chance? Zheljka Nadarević?'

'I go see.'

The girl left the room and Mette wondered at her leaving the cash box there unattended on one of the desks. On an impulse, she opened the little metal chest, to see what sort of income these people were getting. In it were a couple of bills of small denomination, and a good bit of change. Actually, the box contained a surprisingly large heap of change, much of it in twenty-kroner pieces, the most valuable of the more recently minted Norwegian coins. Before she'd given the act or its consequences any thought, Mette picked out all the twenty-kroner pieces, one by one, and dropped them into her raincoat pocket. With trembling fingers, she closed the lid and walked quickly across the room to a corner where a heavy rope had been strung tightly from one wall to the other to hold the metal dry-cleaner hangers on which the used clothing hung. Mette leafed through the clothes, as if she were shopping.

From the doorway came that familiarly accented English. 'Oh. It is you, Mrs Kaldstad. Hasiba said someone asked for me.' It startled Mette to see how exhausted Zheljka looked, maybe not as bony as before but with a queasier skin tone, though she still had that natural elegance of hers. And of course she was still under thirty. Pulling herself to full height, Mette put her hand into the pocket of her raincoat and fingered the coins, like amulets.

'I asked to see you,' she said. 'I . . . I just wondered how the two of you were getting along, it's been months and months. So I thought, as long as I'm here, I could check if you're around. I'm delivering clothes, you see, things Hans Olav and I don't use any more. Good things, really, just that we've both put on weight . . .'

Still in the doorway, neither inside the room nor out, Zheljka looked accusatory, or indifferent. Maybe downright angry. Or was Zheljka just confused?

'Well, Mrs Kaldstad,' Zheljka said finally. 'It is very nice of you. We are doing fine. I work here and Mesud has a job at the print shop at the shopping center. Yes. We are doing quite fine, thank you, very much.'

'Zheljka. There's something I never told you while

you were living at our house, that I kept thinking if you knew it, maybe you'd understand a little better about me, and my husband . . .'

Just then, Hasiba walked back in, seated herself by the bookcases and resumed trying on jewelry, turning one side of her face and then the other to a tiny purple make-up mirror. Mette and Zheljka, meanwhile, remained in their positions, with Mette unable to continue.

'Well,' Mette said finally, 'maybe this isn't a good time to talk. I guess you're working.' She was about to retreat when the weight of the coins in her pocket shifted and she became angry. Why shouldn't she get to explain? Why should she be left feeling guilty and insignificant?

'May I talk to you a minute, alone?'

'Of course. Yes,' Zheljka said and led the way out into the hallway.

Mette closed the classroom door behind them. Why should she be afraid of this younger woman?

'You see,' she began, 'my parents were in Auschwitz, and Bergen-Belsen. You've heard about Auschwitz, haven't you? I mean, Tito didn't keep that information out of the schools or anything did he, the way they did in Austria, about how the Germans exterminated the Jews? Well my parents, we're Jews and my parents were Hungarian Jews, from Budapest, and . . . You see, my father was at the university there when the war came . . .'

Zheljka wasn't looking at her. She had turned

to gaze out the high, horizontal window of the pre-
fabricated hallway; she focused so intently that
Mette's eyes had to follow hers. Perched on a tree
branch visible through that narrow strip of glass, a
magpie shrieked.

Zheljka turned back to Mette, her face frozen but
flushed.

'Do you see, Zheljka?' Mette said to that face. 'Do
you understand what I'm trying to tell you?'

'I do not think I do, Mrs Kaldstad.' Zheljka's
breathing picked up speed.

'Please. Call me *Mette*. You lived in my house.
Please, call me by my name – *Mette*.'

No, Zheljka was not going to make this easier.
Mette began to wonder herself what it was she
wanted. Why was she having this conversation?
'You see, I wanted you to know I understand.'

Zheljka, silent as if she had no intention of responding, did finally speak. 'What is this you think
you understand?'

'Isn't that obvious?'

'Not at all,' Zheljka said, the words leaking out of
her like acid. 'You could be saying you understand
what it was like to be a prisoner of war since your
parents were prisoners. But you were not, and so
you do not.'

'That's not what I mean!'

'No? Maybe then you are telling me you understand why the Croatians were close to the Nazis and
that I should not feel guilty for what my parents did
to your parents. Which I do not. Or . . .' Zheljka

89

seethed now, as if some lid had burned away and there were nothing to contain the pressure. Mette tried to interrupt her, but in vain.

'Or you could want me to pity you, Mrs Kaldstad. Or forgive you . . .'

'No!'

'Or feel that we are just alike, you and me, which we are not.'

'I never did anything bad to you!' Mette gasped. 'Why didn't you let me give you anything when you were at my house?'

'Thank you, very much, for taking us into your home. Do you want more than that?'

'No. Nothing!' Mette dug into her pocket and pulled out a fistful of the refugees' coins and threw them onto the floor. 'Here! Keep them!'

Mette turned to flee but, all at once, there in the schoolhouse doorway, something made sense to her, and for the first time.

'Wait a minute,' she commanded shrilly. Zheljka looked back at her from down the hall. 'You may think I don't understand, but you don't understand either, Zheljka, do you? Who can understand such horrible things? Not even God, I'm sure of it. Not even God understands all this!'

In her car, with the engine idling and the windows shut, Mette wept. Through the fogged windshield she didn't see Zheljka approach, didn't know anyone was out there until she heard the knock at the driver's window. She blew her nose, looked at herself in the rearview mirror and then rolled the window open, just a crack.

Huddled out there in the rain, a heavy blue sweater pulled up over her hair, Zheljka held out some sort of bundle toward the car. Whether her cheeks were wet from rain or tears, Mette couldn't tell. 'Here, Mette. To apologize. Today I am grouchy.'

'Oh.' Mette would not make it easier either.

'Mesud had an accident, you see.'

'Oh!' Now this was something else. 'How sad! Is he okay?'

'He will be fine.' Zheljka pushed the bundle she carried through the open car window. 'Please. Take this – to say I am sorry.'

'Oh, no. You don't have to give me anything!'

'But I want you to have it,' Zheljka insisted, over the sound of the rain.

It was an old shawl of violet velvet with a ragged orange fringe and garish flowers embroidered around its edges. Mette would never have chosen it for herself, yet it looked surprisingly beautiful to her just then. Like home. 'Thank you very much, Zheljka. But really, you don't need to do this.'

'Up here I have been wearing that like a scarf because it is so cold, but I used to keep it on my piano.'

'In Sarajevo?'

'No. I have nothing left from there. In Rome. I had it in Rome, before I came here.'

'I didn't know you were in Rome. Or that you played the piano, either.'

'I studied music when the war came.'

'Oh, Zheljka. You're getting all wet. Please. Get in the car, will you?'

Zheljka glanced back at the schoolhouse for a moment, then ran around the car and got in. Mette turned off the motor and draped the damp shawl neatly over the shoulders of her raincoat.

The two women sat in silence inside the fogged car. Mette played with the hanging orange threads, which made her think of the fringe on her father's *tallis*, the prayer shawl they'd buried him in. She didn't know what to make of the gift.

'I'm sorry too,' Mette said to the clouded windshield and set about untangling the fringe, string by string, imagining the shawl lying across Zheljka's piano in Rome.

'Rome,' Mette said at last. 'That's such a romantic city. Hans Olav and I went there once. All those narrow alleys, so charming.'

Zheljka looked at her with a smile Mette couldn't interpret. *Enigmatic*, Mette said to herself as she played with her wedding ring, turning it around and around. Being a refugee in Rome sounded to her like a contradiction in terms.

'That trip to Italy,' she began, 'Hans Olav and I used to go all over, for a while, to lots of places. On vacations. You see, I can't get pregnant and we thought, you know, maybe we could fool my body into relaxing. Sort of like what happens to couples when they adopt a baby, or maybe get a puppy, and suddenly she's pregnant. We really relaxed in Rome . . . But it didn't help.'

Zheljka's silence continued. Hailstones bounced off the car. When Mette put her hand in her coat pocket to get her gloves, her fingers found the remaining coins. Why had she stolen them? That was what she did, she said to herself accusingly: steal.

'How about if we go out to lunch together,' Mette blurted out, 'please, as my guest? Right now.' She looked at her watch. It was only ten thirty in the morning.

Zheljka took so long to answer, Mette thought she hadn't heard; the hail rattled the roof.

'I cannot do it today, I am afraid,' Zheljka said at last. 'There is only me and Hasiba in the shop today.'

'Couldn't we plan it, then? Couldn't I pick you up some other day? I'd really like to give you something, Zheljka.'

Again that strange smile. Did Zheljka know?

Zheljka reached into her own pocket just then and brought out a handful of coins. Mette gasped, sure she'd been caught. 'I almost forgot,' Zheljka said, in what seemed a perfectly normal tone of voice. 'Here is the money you . . . dropped on the floor in there.' It looked to Mette to be even more than the amount she had thrown down.

'No. No. Consider it a donation. I was just angry.'

'We are not charity cases here, Mrs Kaldstad. We work for our money,' Zheljka retorted, her face stern.

'Take this. Go inside and buy something from our store if you want us to have it.' She held out her hand filled with the coins. Mette could not but accept back her burden.

'But what about lunch?' she persisted.

Zheljka turned away. Then she shrugged her shoulders. 'Next Thursday, maybe? I will not be alone here that day. But *I* will pay. You will be *my* guest, otherwise I will not come.'

This was not what Mette had in mind at all. But what choice did she have now?

At home, Mette emptied her coat pockets onto her polished mahogany bedroom bureau, then threw the coat onto the bed. There were seventeen twenty-kroner pieces, a total of three hundred and forty kroner. A lot of money. Enough for a medium-priced pair of shoes, or for Chinese food for two, if Hans Olav didn't order any beer. She made three neat piles of five coins each, and one of two. She made two piles of six and one of five, then eight piles of two and one of only one . . . But it was useless. Seventeen is a prime number, she remembered from her school days; there's no way to divide it evenly.

The coins were heavy and big, golden in color but not made of gold. Hadn't Zheljka wondered what she was doing with so many twenty-kroner pieces? Maybe Zheljka and Hasiba, tallying their income at the end of the day, would notice that exactly three hundred and forty kroner were missing. Maybe by their lunch date on Thursday Zheljka might have figured it out. But would that *enigmatic*, angry woman tell her if she knew?

What was she to do with these coins? All the tellers at her bank knew her. Stores would certainly comment on a customer paying with so much change. She saw the shawl Zheljka had given her still wrapped around the shoulders of her coat which lay on her bed. Mette unfolded it neatly, embroidered side down, and smiled as she combed and stroked the ragged fringe into some semblance of order. She piled on all the coins and tied the shawl, corner to corner, like a hobo's bag. Mette kissed the bundle lightly. Then, she shoved it to the very back of her underwear drawer, behind the lace lavender sachets, and behind the pastel-peach satin slip from Steen & Strøm, still with its price tags because the one she'd taken was too small. And behind the stack of the initialed handkerchiefs her mother had bought her for each birthday. That had been the only sort of luxury item Mette's mother permitted herself – something useful. And behind the little bag of assorted, ugly, multi-colored plastic earrings she'd taken the week before from the drug store at her neighborhood shopping center. Her heart felt explosive.

When she closed her underwear drawer, Mette had that familiar sense that the whole bureau glowed, conspicuously.

That night she had a dream. She was about seven, riding with an elderly couple in a rusted motor-home.

The driver, the man, stopped and pushed Mette out, alone, onto a vast tundra. As she shivered there, a small bird attempting to penetrate the frozen ground with its beak suddenly unearthed a golden object. Cocking its head from side to side, it presented to Mette all its many facets. She grabbed for it, but the bird lifted its beak and swallowed. On its way down, the object's sharp edges split the bird's throat like a razor, exposing wet flesh, muscle and bone, which glittered in the icy wind.

Mette awoke, sweating, and pressed her body as tightly against her husband's as possible, given that he slept with his back turned toward her.

Don't Call Me Miriam

Mette got impetigo once: she had fallen down on a class field trip – she never did master the Norwegian art of hiking in the mountains – and the scrape got infected. The scab kept building up and Mette remembered looking at it, thinking, *My whole life feels just like that – crusty, like a big scab on a sore.* That's what Mette had wanted Zheljka to understand there in the hallway of the refugee resale store. She knew she'd have to find another picture, though: scabs don't make you seem at all heroic.

What if she told her about all those nightmares in the air? Or how behind every joke her father ever told was somebody's horrible death; even now, Mette couldn't hear people laugh without listening for the scream.

Or about how *Mette* was just her name in Norway; her real name was *Miriam*, though only her mother ever called her that. Jews name their kids after dead relatives and Miriam was an aunt, her mother's little fourteen-year-old sister, whom a blond guard at Auschwitz kicked and clubbed and beat till he felt satisfied she was dead. And she did die too – in Mette's mother's arms. What a namesake. Mette could swear that every time her mother called out *Miriam* she could hear hob-nailed boots crushing bones.

Or, maybe, she should just tell her about that one afternoon, when she came back from another hiking tour. Not that she fell down a mountain or got raped or something like that, not that anything big really happened.

Just that no matter how she tried, Mette's muscles never got Norwegian-strong; they were always *slappe*, the word is pronounced *shlahp-eh* so it sounds like what it means – sloppy, floppy. Jews weren't skiers like the goyim, Mette's father insisted, they weren't drunks like them (*Oy,oy,oy – shikker ist ein goy*, that was a song he sang), they didn't beat their wives or think real life started only once you died. Their men studied Talmud and argued with God.

He warned Mette, more than once, not to break the chain of tradition. According to Mette's father's logic, assimilation equaled death. To her, though, assimilation didn't seem fatal, simply impossible.

But she tried nonetheless. She went on all those hiking trips with kids from her class. And after one such day in the mountains doing her best to keep up, fat little her with those *slappe* muscles, everyone went over to Marit's house. Mette was fourteen then.

The land around the farmhouse Marit lived in

had several *uthus* on it, those one-room cabins old Norwegian farmhouses all have around them, with tall door-sills and short doors and tiny windows, and everything unpainted pine. Marit's parents let the kids have an *uthus* to themselves, complete with posters of Jean-Paul Belmondo and Brigitte Bardot, and a 45 rpm record-player.

Not just girls from the class were there, but Marit's older brothers too, plus their friends. Boys. Tall, strong, blond boys, the kind about whom Mette's mother would mumble, 'Here come the Hitler *Jugend*!' whenever they passed on the street looking so proud and walking so unswervingly that Mette and her mother had to separate, each to her own side of the sidewalk, and let them pass.

Even on a late spring day like that one Mette wore a long-sleeved shirt so the ragged, scabby eczema skin on her arms wouldn't show. In a recurring nightmare of hers, the eczema crept up her neck and onto her face like spiders, though, in reality, her face usually stayed clear of eczema. Not clear of teenage acne, however, which was another scab story it wouldn't help to tell to Zheljka.

But if Zheljka could just have seen her that day – though Mette cringed, looking back at herself – sitting with her knees pulled up to her chest on the smooth pine floor, her back against the itchy khaki blanket that covered the sofa . . . upon which sat: gorgeous Per Mikkelsen, the *Goy Boy*. From across the room came the grunts and whoops of Per's friends' wrestling and the thumping beat of the

'Blacksmith Blues'. And all the while Per's athletic thigh brushed, again and again, against Mette's face – her hot, red face – and the heat of his body pulsed off his grass-stained pants leg, wafting into her nostrils the dark, male odor of cigarettes and sweat.

Mette kept on trying to stick some comment or other into blue-eyed Per's conversation, something that would seem normal and regular and charming, and gentile. Finally, when she made some fart joke, something that got everybody to laugh, it happened: Per took his big blond hand and ruffled her glued-down-with-hairspray hair. Oh, her joy!

She remembered looking down just after that. On the floor by Per's feet, next to the beer bottle he used for an ashtray, lay his cigarette lighter. Mette took it. She took his lighter, a Zippo, a *man's* lighter, an uncircumcised lighter. She slid it into her own pocket where she warmed it with her hand against her thigh. He was so tall.

The real reason she wished she could tell Zheljka all this was so she'd see what it was like for Mette to come dancing home after all that. Home – into the gray-beige air of their two-bedroom third-floor apartment, with glass in the windows so old and scratched that the sun couldn't look shiny, not even in May. This wasn't the place where the loo was in the courtyard, where they lived when she was little. This one had the bathroom indoors, though they still had to go outside the apartment and down to the landing between the second and third floors to a toilet they shared with the neighbors, and the father of that family drank, and puked (*Oy,oy,oy . . .*) – yet another story.

When she came home that day, her mother sat right where Mette knew she'd find her, at the square pine table in her perfectly clean kitchen with her back to the window and her hands in her lap, her two feet on the floor, flat. Her legs weren't crossed. Her hands weren't folded. Her mouth wasn't open. Her eyes weren't closed. Nothing. And when the woman saw her daughter, she just stared at the girl's face for one long second and then went back to gazing off into the perpetually dusky light of their apartment without saying a word.

It was always like that. Always, ever since Mette was born.

So Mette left the kitchen. On her way through the hall to her bedroom, she noticed her mother's purse lying open on the mahogany table, on the doily stained yellow from some leaky flower vase. Mette left it alone this time, though, hell, it was her right to take anything she needed seeing as how they never gave it. She went into her own room and sat on the bed, on the crocheted bedspread that always slid off the slippery blanket below. She took Per's Zippo from her pocket and practiced flipping open the lid and rolling the wheel to get it to light, trying to do it his way, so both those movements flowed together smoothly, as if they were one.

Parting the Darkness

clouds . . .

Mesud is cloudy, morphined and pillowsoft, not in this hospital room, not in Norway after the accident at the print shop, but in the bedroom in the morning, back in Sarajevo, before the other kids were born and he had to be a big boy. Now he's still little, Mama's fleshy arms hold him, his face on her breast, he can smell her talcum fragrance as she scratches his back, just where it itches, her groggy voice crooning, *Medo, little bear, my little boy.*

Mama, I'm thirsty, and the nurse wipes his lips with a spongy stick. His eyes are now open and it's daytime and here's Zheljka, *I love you, Zheljka, forgive me* . . . His eyes close again and the morphine takes over, takes him up and to the right on the tree swing, a braided rope knotted through a plank that you sit on and swing up to the rooftops, treetops, clouds . . .

. . . he floats on them softly where pain never was, tears never held back, soldiering dead, no bullets or grenades, and the color red is sticky and that gurgling screaming choking, with the inside of you cramping from a voice inside your belly that says, *Mama, I'm so sorry . . .*

. . . about my brother, Mirsad, I pinned him to the ground and my knee is on his chest and I count until he gives in, until he gasps I GIVE. I know he can't breathe and I'm glad he's so little. YOU GIVE? I want from him I GIVE and when I get it, let him up, check to see if Mama saw me and I'll lie if he snitches. This time's like that, only worse, so much worse – it's not my knee, he's not my brother, he's never getting up, this time there is no GIVING, he will never get up again and I still look back over my shoulder but Mama's nowhere to be found, I'm a man, he's my Enemy. They call this War, you see I had to, Mother, forgive me, they're our Enemies, they are the Serbs – yes, I know, just like your mother, just like Baka, *she was Serbian but don't tell them. You mustn't tell that to anyone,* Majko, *promise me, no one. Ever.*

He groans now and the nurse comes and injects more blessed morphine into the tube that leads to the needle on the back of Mesud's hand and the clouds . . .

the clouds . . .

all kind, dry and sweet like flowers *like you, Zheljka, in my arms when we lived in that apartment. Careful, sweetheart, I'll take care of you. Don't hurt yourself, fragrant Zheljka, I will keep you from all harm, have only softness now and safety . . .*

and Mesud sleeps . . .

and dreams of neon, flashing black around the

window, pushing his body into the corner of his mind where he crouches, can't breathe under that force that has him huddled under its weight, glaring at him, faceless. Then it has a face, yes, it has a face. Just look who's keeping him prisoner, look who's there beside his bed – that little boy's face, whose face is that?

He awakens, but into clouds, opens his eyes and sees his father, the broad squat back, the bulging shirt, the balding patch. *Turn around, Babo, let me see you.* But *Babo* isn't living. *Am I dead then, like he is, from the burning of their pliers, dying young just like my father, leaving a wife and many children? Only I haven't any children, have no children have no children . . .*

Not that kid, that one named Zero. He's no boy. A monster. She grew their monster in her belly (he was little, so afraid, those skinny arms like tree twigs, always carrying a cap gun and I saw him in the alley when his mother talked to strangers who could take the fucking bastard, take him, take him off my hands, what kind of father am I?)

I have to stop these pictures, I'm still digging out their trenches, still their prisoner in that playground like the one when we were children, they sardine us, never feed us, make us dig out all their trenches. I know these guys, I know them, all my life I've always known them. 'Hey guys, it's me. It's Mesud.' But they come and take me anyhow, drag me in there by my . . .

Mesud is screaming but now they cannot help him – too soon for so much morphine, his breath already short, Zheljka is beside him swabbing water on his lips, stroking his forehead like a mother, she's a mother, he's a son, and he wasn't there to protect her, left her alone and went off fighting, then when he finally found her, he made her choose between them: *You can have Zero or you can have me.*

Zheljka strokes him slowly, his brow slowly unfurrows and sleep comes to Mesud, Mama's *Medo*, little bear, sleeping sweetly under morphine after the accident at the Norwegian print shop, where he finally got a job, then got caught up in the gears of the machine that folds the paper, a thousand sheets a minute, the one he loved to drum on to the rhythm of the folding, the music of the print shop, rhythm in his groin,

but this time he was careless, it can crush you that machine, crush any careless idiot who lets his shirt-sleeves flutter. It splayed him like their Jesus, slammed him up against the metal, bashed and clamped him, broke his arm and snapped a rib that punctured a lung which they say will probably heal. He was lucky. He was glad, glad to be finally wounded, knowing he deserved it, at last, punished, this stocky tender soldier who deserted his whole country when he hitched with a UN convoy after the Serbs let him go, when they dumped off their prisoners like so much garbage across the lines, he fled to Split, to a refugee camp, didn't head back to Sarajevo to find his Division to help them murder more old friends. Way back at the beginning he could have hidden from conscription, never

106

abandoned Zheljka, been there to save her, his mother and his sisters, not left them all alone, never rescuing anyone and with no children to his name,

and his father died too early before the boy could know him in a country without safety, leaving a wife and all those children; little Mesud was the eldest. His mother sat him down, *Mesud, you're the man now.* He was only thirteen, hadn't yet begun to grow, he grew strong but never tall. He took care of all those children by working in a print shop. Where he learned very early that he should always roll up his sleeves.

Mesud lightens as the morphine levels off, as the cells weave up new bone mass and the rib begins to mend and the lung begins inflating and time moves slowly forward. Then the clouds thin, his head clears, his mind parts the darkness and his eyes begin to see:

He was nothing very special. A plain old-fashioned soldier warring against his neighbors for a salary of cigarettes, lying low behind the bushes, shooting without looking. Then when they declared the cease-fires to gather up their corpses, sharing smokes with Serbs, asking one another to carry greetings home to loved ones still alive on the other side's terrain: *Tell my mother I'm okay*, then they recommenced their shooting.

Think of something else, Mesud hears himself mumble. *How about the park at Igman. Or Mama's stew with apricots. The minarets at prayertime, or*

*your smallest sister newborn. No, don't picture
Zheljka pregnant . . .*

*But at the outdoor café, the music in your belly,
those girls from the Conservatory, hot numbers on
high heels, prancing stretchpant asses and those
luscious little tits, Zheljka walking by, pretending to
ignore you, her nostrils all a-twitch and her eyes
on fire with challenge. Silky Zheljka on that bed
when the bird flew in and slammed itself against the
plastered ceiling, and you knew that you could save
it, you could help to set it free . . .*

*Think about playing with your brothers in the forest
up on Igman. When you found that German helmet in
a Second World War trench . . .*

*Not these trenches! Get out of these other trenches.
Out!*

*. . . Yes, go back to that helmet which you put up
on a boulder and your brothers took turns stoning
it, laughing, yelling, until . . . Mirsad, little Mirsad,
he was seven, took a stick and bashed the helmet,
knocked it to the ground, kicked, kicked, spitting,
screaming 'Četnik, fucking Četnik' – furious at the
helmet. All that hate? Just think about it. All that
hate. From where? They were your friends, then your
torturers who talked to you nicely when you were
alone but as soon as the others came into the room
they spat on you, cursed at you, showed off for their
buddies. Where does it come from, all that hate?*

*I can't think about that now, find something else
instead . . .*

Like the print shop, where it wasn't words that

mattered, but the smell of all those fluids and the colors on your fingers and the rhythm of the presses and the order of the pages, it was the music that you loved . . .

and the knife that cuts the paper—

No! Not the knives, you know which knives, the knives they used to carve you, Mesud don't think that stink, their cigarettes burning your chest, your face caked over with your own dried shit – Mesud, change the pictures! Crush your brow, squeeze your eyelids, clench your jaw, change the pictures—

Think of something else!

I can't. It's always with me under everything I see, behind every pretty landscape there it is, that crazy neighbor heating pliers,

like the ones I'd fix my car with, yes, my car. I remember, the little Yugo, I put in fleece upholstery and the distance I could travel on a single tank of gas . . .

To the park up on Mount Igman, Zheljka brought a picnic and her little music player – yes, this thought is better – and the tapes of classical music she wanted me to love and I'd tease her about it, sing her songs of Sarajevo, teach her songs from home. Remember by the river at that little dark café where we waited for the others – one of them named Drago, wait . . . It was that Drago Zheljka said was Komandant, don't think don't think don't think . . .

you're sleepy, let the sleep just take you over so the pictures won't keep coming, think of Zheljka's velvet hips, her holding you and singing one of her great composer songs, Zheljka in bed in the morning and you nuzzling her breasts, and all the ease she hasn't *got now. I can hardly hold her like a man now, she can hardly let me inside her, hardly needs me any more.*

If only I could sleep, please let me sleep. Yes.

And Mesud slept.

Until the evening. Once again they cut his dosage, and the clouds thinned out some more.

Zheljka, he said when he saw her. *Do you hate me?*

What? she said.

For being such a coward?

You're drugged, and foolstupid.

I would have saved you if I could. There's so much I've never told you. You were young when we got married. And I thought I was a man.

Hush, rest now, Mesud. It's over. We can talk about it later.

Talk. Mama's dead. They murdered Majko, Zheljka, it hurts me when I breathe.

Shhh, now rest, Mesud. You'll be all right, the doctor told me, you're going to be fine.

She caressed him. He closed his eyes and rested but knew she bore resentment, could feel the small reserve in the words she didn't say. Like how she never called him *Medo* any more.

Zheljka, he cried, but it was night-time. No one was there except other patients. One of them snored, another one rattled, a third, yelling in Norwegian, must have told Mesud to shut up. Zheljka wasn't there now. He was alone. And the clouds, ahh, the clouds,

were they gone?

110

Theft

Dressing for their Thursday lunch, Mette wondered if Zheljka would be offended she wasn't wearing the violet shawl. She could say she'd placed it on their piano, though what if they ended up coming back to the house and Zheljka saw it wasn't there? Odd that Zheljka never touched that piano all those weeks she and Mesud had lived with them. But then, Mette never touched it any more either. Her parents more or less forced her to take piano lessons as a kid, the piano being one of her mother's luxurious, useful gifts. Once she grew up, she never played except when they asked her to. Now they were dead.

She decided to drive Zheljka to lunch close to Vigeland Park, a sculpture garden, an Oslo tourist attraction that Zheljka maybe hadn't seen. Besides, a café near there was fairly cheap so Zheljka wouldn't spend much on their lunch. Mette ate a large sandwich before leaving home because she knew how her hunger could overpower her will.

*　　　*　　　*

During the car-ride Zheljka said nothing, so Mette babbled on like a tour-guide about Vigeland and his statues, about how Teutonic they seemed and how provocative that became after the German occupation of Norway.

'Yes,' Zheljka said. 'I know.'

'Have you been to the park before?'

'Yes, I have,' she said, then turned away.

'Didn't you love that statue of the two-year-old throwing a tantrum?' Mette asked when again she could bear Zheljka's silence no longer. 'My favorites though are the ones down by the lake, the littlest bronze babies, creeping, and playing with their toes and learning to sit up? They're so cute, don't you think? I always get teary when I see all those baby statues.'

'I did not stay down there long,' Zheljka responded. 'It stank from all the ducks and gulls.'

They took no tour of the park to view the sculptures but proceeded directly to the white wooden café, newly reopened as the long winter neared its end.

They sat at a table for four, facing each other, each claiming an empty chair on which to pile her coat and purse. Zheljka ordered an open sandwich of thinly sliced smoked salmon on a mound of cold scrambled eggs, but Mette chose something less expensive, and less fattening: a small salad.

'I want to apologize for yelling when you were at the center,' Zheljka began.

'No. No. You see . . .'

'Let me finish. Mesud was in an accident at his work.'

'You told me. Is he all right?'

'He is fine now, back at his job again.' Zheljka scrutinized Mette a moment. 'You know, I forget sometimes that people like you, people who have a life in one place and with peace, that you too have your problems. I remember my troubles before the war, how big they seemed to me, I have to laugh. Like this accident now. It was nothing.'

'Zheljka, I don't know anything about you from before you came here.'

'Oh, I had a fine life before the war. You have been in Dubrovnik, no?'

'No,' Mette admitted.

'It is an ancient city and in the old section the streets are paved with big stones that are worn so smooth they shine.' Zheljka seemed to warm to her subject, becoming surprisingly animated.

'And there is music, each year a festival where the very best musicians – violinists, pianists – they come to play and we students, we could meet them. We followed them to restaurants, outside on roof gardens because the nights were so warm, the air was soft like a fruit. And they flirted with us, those old guys, and we had them buying us dinner – fish fresh from the Adriatic, I can smell it now, with lemon and vine-ripened tomatoes – and talking to us about music, advising us about our boyfriends. I am telling you. How I cried for Dubrovnik when I moved to Sarajevo.'

'But what happened then? In the war?'

Zheljka looked at her so intensely Mette felt pinned, pushed up against some wall. 'I lived *before* the war too, you know. I studied at the Sarajevska Muziçka Akademija. I played a student concert once, in front of two hundred people. Just because we came here with nothing does not mean we came from nothing. I had everything you have – a washing machine, a coffee maker to plug in, little cups with gold along the rim, white porcelain you could almost see through. I had a life before I was a refugee. But you are not interested. When I was in the refugee camp, people like you visited because they were curious. They bribed the Red Cross or the UN soldiers or somebody to get them into the war zone – "war-tourists", we called them. That is what you remind me of.'

'No! That wasn't what I meant. You twist my words.' It was true, though: Mette hadn't pictured Zheljka with a coffee maker and fine cups. In her mind, she saw an upright piano, dusty and scratched, with yellowed, broken keys, and on it that vulgar shawl, its shabby orange fringe like a mouth full of rotten teeth. Then she remembered the coins wrapped safely inside it.

'All I'm trying to say is you're not the only one with pain.'

Zheljka sighed, put her elbows on the table and rubbed her eyes slowly with upturned palms. 'Excuse me,' she said, pushing her chair back from the table, 'I need to use the WC.'

Mette was alone. Her eyes wandered to Zheljka's full plate; she had hardly touched her food. Mette filched a piece of smoked salmon and swallowed it virtually unchewed. Then her glance landed on the empty chair to her right, the one containing Zheljka's coat – and her purse, an open pouch made of different-colored leathers. Sticking up into view was Zheljka's wallet. With no forethought, Mette reached over and took it out, clicking it open. Her hands sweat as she leafed through sections holding neither a driver's license nor bank cards nor credit cards, but only two one-hundred-kroner bills and a few coins. Mette didn't know what she was looking for until, when she pulled out Zheljka's Croatian passport, with a golden crown on the dark blue checkerboard cover, she knew she'd found it: a picture of Zheljka. So young Zheljka looked, such a short time ago. With fingers stiffened by adrenaline, Mette slid the passport down into her pants pocket. She succeeded in shoving Zheljka's wallet back into the gaping purse just in time.

Zheljka returned looking even paler than before.

'Shall we have some dessert?' Mette asked, searching the menu for something sweet. She was still hungry.

'Not for me, thank you. I need something to settle my stomach.' Zheljka asked the waitress for crackers and sparkling water.

Mette ordered nothing.

As Zheljka seemed to have no plans to speak,

Mette tried to remember what they'd been talking about before Zheljka left. 'You were going to tell me about your life during the war.'

'Look, can we not talk about something neutral, Mrs Kaldstad? Something that does not remind us of our differences.'

'But I keep trying to tell you,' Mette complained, 'we aren't so different!'

'Maybe you are right. Maybe I just feel I have gone too far. Outside of the human race. Maybe I am just flattering myself.'

'Yes. Maybe!' Mette grabbed greedily at the thread of Zheljka's admission. Now, finally, was her chance to explain. 'I told you at the center about my parents in the war, remember? Auschwitz and Bergen-Belsen? Well, I grew up with that every single day. My father's tattoo nobody ever mentioned. And all that screaming at night.'

Mette told how her father's nightmares would awaken her, how she'd go into her parents' room to ask, *What's wrong with Daddy?* only to be led by her mother, in silence, back to her own bed.

Zheljka sipped her water then chewed a cracker slowly, her eyes seeming to study the blue and white squares of the tablecloth.

'But me,' Mette kept on, 'well, I wasn't supposed to have any pain at all. I was the hope for the future, the lucky one. *Mother's little singing lark,* she called me. To you, all that might seem like no big deal, like nothing,' she protested, 'but really – a fat and clutzy teenage girl with black eyebrows growing straight across her forehead, with a nose that didn't turn up at all, and with kinky hair that wasn't anywhere near blonde – in Norway. And this girl didn't just have eczema, she had acne too, and for her to be a Jew on top of it, getting bullied, and hearing them whisper *Christ killer* and *Jew pig* – well, was that really nothing? Is anybody laughing? Are you laughing?'

Zheljka stroked the beads of condensation down the side of her glass in stripes.

'But hell!' Mette cried. 'What's scabs and acne compared to concentration camps and gas chambers, right? And now you're telling me exactly the same thing. What do I know? Well, I know a lot, Zheljka. Quite a lot!'

At this, Mette rose, pulled herself to full height and, crossing the restaurant to where the waitress stood sneaking a cigarette and laughing, she ordered herself a slice of apple tart, heated – and with *two* scoops of vanilla ice cream on top.

Neither one spoke as Mette ate her dessert. When Zheljka finally broke the silence, though her voice sounded soft, the vein on her throat pulsed visibly.

'I am sorry, Mrs Kaldstad . . .'

'*Mette!* Please! Call me *Mette!*'

'. . . I am sorry,' Zheljka continued quietly, eyes downcast, fingers following the edge of her spoon around and around, 'but you do not know what you do not know. And you could be a little more – what is the word – "humble". Yes, that is it: "humble"

117

about what you do not know about human suffering.'

Zheljka took the last sip of her sparkling water and seemed to make a decision. 'I am going to tell you a story now, not because of pity. This is no contest of who hurts worse. No. I just want to show you that not everything can be survived. I will only give you the bones of the story and you will have to imagine the rest.'

Mette crossed her arms and legs, tilted her head to one side and pursed her lips. But she did listen.

'A war starts,' Zheljka began, in an exaggerated sing-song as if speaking to a child, 'and a young woman's new husband is taken away to fight. She tries to flee but is taken prisoner. Then she is . . . taken. Many times, by many men, for months. Somehow, she catches no disease. But they do make her pregnant. When they are sure it is too late for an abortion, they let her go. And she has that baby, a boy, and at the hospital they will not let her kill him. So she keeps him. Who knows why. She keeps him. "Zero", she names him . . .'

Mette nearly interrupted to ask if 'Zero' was a common Croatian name, but she decided to keep quiet.

'And slowly the two of them . . . No. I will not tell that part. I skip until later. This lady and the boy, they escape to Italy. And when the boy is four, this woman's husband shows up again – she thought he was dead. The husband, he does not want his enemies' child. No, sir, he does not want it. And so,

what does the woman do? She gives the boy away.
The End. Or, wait: we say, she "gives him up for
adoption", that is nicer, no?'

The image Mette saw before her was Zheljka
handing the child to her and Hans Olav, the boy's
little hand being placed in her own, how she would
pick him up and hold him in her empty arms, her
adopted son. 'You gave him up?'

'*I* gave him up? I told you, this is a story.'

But Mette had been struck by the realization that
if there was this one boy, then there must be more
babies like him to be had. 'How did you do that?'

'You mean, how could I do such a thing? You
think you could have done anything different?'

'No. I really mean – *how*? Is there an agency? Did
someone come and pick him up? Did you take him
somewhere?'

Perhaps, Mette thought later, Zheljka did trust her
after all. Or maybe she was just caught off guard?
For whatever reason, Mette's question seemed to
grab Zheljka like a hook, dragging her into the
tunnel of her story and not releasing her until she
had told it all.

'I dressed him in his little shorts,' she said quietly,
her eyes focused on the past. 'They came down to
his knees and his thighs were so skinny inside those
big cuffs. I combed his hair and he looked at me in
the mirror, serious, as if he knew something was
wrong. I was not crying any more, I was gone to that
place I can go, an empty place where everything
except my body is gone. I was gone. Otherwise I

would not have been able to do it. I brushed his hair with a wet brush, so it would lie down flat across his tiny temple, his four-year-old forehead had wrinkles like an old man; he was looking at me in the mirror as I wetted and brushed his hair. I smoothed it and smoothed it.'

Mette watched the pictures Zheljka's words created, at first as if she were there with the boy, but gradually as if she and Zero were one.

' "Mama? Where are we going?" Zero asked me.

' "Hush," I said. "Put on your shirt." I had ironed it, a cowboy shirt, his favorite, with horses and lassos on the front. I held Zero with one hand and his suitcase with the other. Mesud knew today was the day and I made him stay away, he was outside Rome somewhere, I have no idea, anywhere, just not near via del Pozzuolo.

' "Wait, Mama," Zero said to me, "I have to take my cap gun!"

'I told him I had packed it. "It is in your bag," I said.

' "I want it now, in my *pocket*." He began to cry.

' "No, we are in a hurry." I almost yelled at him.

' "But I want it, Mama!"

'I stopped and got out his small toy pistol with the plastic white handle. He put it deep into the pocket of his shorts and wiped tears from his face with his arm.

'We walked to the corner. There was a well-dressed couple. The front of my body walked forward, but all my insides and the back of me were screaming "No!" and running in all directions. So I forced my eyes to see the faces of every one of them, what shall I call them? I will not take that word "fathers" into my mouth, after everything they put in my mouth. I saw each of "them", forced myself to look into the eyes of each one I had seen as he did that to me. I placed each one of "them" in front of me to keep my body walking forward and my hand still holding the hand of this little boy, my Zero.

'There stood that fancy couple, he was hardly taller than she was – Italians – he was in a gray jacket, his hand holding his wife's, and she almost cried, but also smiled, even if she tried to cover it up. I hate her. I walk right up to them, I take Zero's hand and I put it into the hand of the woman and I take the suitcase and put it into the hand of the man and I say, "Go!" And I should have stopped there. I was choking, the back of me and the insides were wiping out the front, I was choking on screams that wanted to come out so I pulled myself from me, I pushed myself outside of me, up, up and over the roofs of the alleyway, into the sun that never made it to the cobblestones below. "Go!" I said.

'But right then Zero yanks his hand from the woman's, he drops his pistol, and throws his arms around my hips. "Mama, I want to go home!" He is crying. I reach behind me to pry one finger at a time loose from me, but when I have gotten them loose, those twisting hands, they grab at my thigh and those legs wind around my ankles, like snakes.

'The man spoke Italian. I do not know what he

said. It was rough on the bottom with something fake all over the top of it, and all the time he is using his force to take Zero from me. Zero is kicking and screaming, "Mama, Mama, Mama!"

'I start backing up. If I turn to go, my spine would explode and I could not go through with it so I back up and that person picks Zero up, he kicks and bites and cries, and the woman tries to give him back his gun, pleading with him – pathetic bitch – and I am backing away while they get into a car, a big, expensive, fat, dark sedan, a new car, a rich infertile people's child-stealing car. And I keep backing up; and disappearing up and up and up until they have driven away.

'Zero is still screaming.'

The two women sat as if paralyzed. Then, for one brief moment, their eyes met and the incinerated, inconsolable gaze Mette saw before her she recognized. In that moment, she was looking once again into her own father's nightmare eyes, eyes that see nothing but pain.

Reflexively, Mette reached across the table to place her hands on top of Zheljka's, to comfort her. Something about the gesture, though, felt very wrong, and almost immediately she withdrew.

Silence reigned at that table, as ghosts rustled in the two empty chairs.

Mette closed her eyes hoping to escape what her mind's eye had just seen. But there, projected onto the screen of her inner eyelids, disjointed fragments of facts alluded to or withheld, facts and questions which had floated homelessly all through Mette's life, began aligning themselves into a new pattern in her mind.

Mette's eyes flew open: her mother and father had never told her their whole story, she'd never gotten the timing straight. Her parents said they'd first met in a DP camp and she knew exactly when Bergen-Belsen was liberated. She could count back from her birth to an approximate date of conception . . . if, that is, they'd told her her true date of birth. There were no records, that much she knew, and so no knowing for sure when or where she had been conceived. Here it was, the real question dawning on her: who was really her father? Could it be? Could she, Mette, be the child of an assault? Could she be another Zero?

The question was bold, wild: had they done to her mother what they did to Zheljka? Mette's entire system came alive to this thought. She could hear the clicking in her brain of tens, perhaps hundreds, of realigning associations; the feeling was really quite pleasurable. What if she were half-Jew, half-Nazi? Her blood churned as if hurling its newly polarized genetic components into infinite space.

Mette stared straight ahead and tried to think rationally: she herself had brown hair but her mother's hair had been black. And her father's? His went gray in the camps, so it was hard to tell. Her mother survived both Auschwitz and Bergen-Belsen while still young and pretty. What did she have to do to come out alive? And why had Mette never thought about all this before?

Maybe this was why Mette was an only child. Maybe this explained all those years of silence, that her father never really spoke to her. *Maybe he wasn't her father at all.* He might actually have wished she'd never been born, had even tried to get her mother to give her up for adoption. Well, would she have preferred that? To have grown up far away from all that horror, always there, never spoken about? To have had other parents?

A rare cramp of longing hit her. How seldom Mette let herself miss her mother and father, how fast she'd quit mourning their deaths. During her thirties she would proclaim, hoping to sound crass, that you couldn't miss two people who, when they were alive, were too busy being Holocausted to even notice you. But that wasn't true at all. Not at all. For her, their destinies belonged to the Great Events of History; their lives definitely mattered. It was her own she could never be sure of. Until now.

Quite suddenly, that paradox struck her. In a flash, Mette caught a glimpse of herself from the outside. There she was, wishing, truly hoping, that her mother had been sexually violated and that her father wasn't her father at all. The absurdity of wanting that brought Mette round from her feverish inquiry, and back to Zheljka sitting opposite her.

'Don't you get it?' Mette burst out, as if Zheljka had been following her entire internal train of thought. 'All my life I've thought I don't count because nothing horrible and historical happened to me. But that can't be true.' Mette's hand in her pocket clutched at Zheljka's passport. 'Zheljka, you're more than just raped – you're the mother of Zero. Zero matters.'

Mette smiled widely as Zheljka stared at her, blinking and blinking. Mette felt how her bodyheat warmed the passport there in her pocket and that feeling gave her immense joy. She even considered sliding it right back across the table into Zheljka's empty hands.

Forensic Evidence

I had no choice, Beate, I had to look. I'd gotten this letter saying they wanted me at the war crimes trials. The Tribunal in The Hague had Drago in custody – the *Komandant*, our neighbor with that big dog – and they knew I was one of the women he'd held in that camp. So, one night when all the others left the store, I pulled down the shades, locked the doors, unplugged the phone in the schoolroom where all the used clothes hang. It's not that I hadn't seen myself in a mirror since it happened, I just never looked for proof before.

I took off my olive corduroy donated pants, and the navy sweatshirt, all worn out and probably American, with one of those awful smile faces on it – two pin-prick eyes and a slashed mouth. Propped up in the corner, the store's full-length mirror tilts making you look taller and thinner than for real, which probably doesn't hurt our sales any. But it's so light and cheap it bends you in the middle, fun-housey and scoliotic.

Now I was down to my bra and underpants. I

never used to wear a bra, but the feeling of bouncing, that sensation of the weightless moment when my breasts, even tiny ones like mine, fly up, flings my memory back to you know when and I break out in a cold sweat. So now I wear a bra, even though I can't breathe and I used to be fond of breathing.

My underpants – well, mine now – are dirty-white cotton, thick old-lady things. But then, honestly, Beate, can you picture me putting on some lacy affair, dressing it up? Gift-wrapping it?

I had my hair in this huge purple plastic clip that gapes like shark jaws when you squeeze it, and when you let it go it clumps up the hair, grabs at it, like they did.

Yes, I know what you're thinking, that I could hardly have made myself less attractive. Brilliant.

It was early spring which at home would mean wild flowers and fragrance, but up here was just brown slush and rotting snow. And roof-avalanches – when that Nordic excuse for a sun warms the roof tiles enough, a winter's worth of snow slides off in one fat heavy sheet, stripping the housetop naked, God help whoever's caught underneath, and when that snow sheet slides the rumbling of it grinds so deep it vibrates your belly long before your ears even know they're hearing. Which is what happened right then: just as I was getting up my courage to check out my damaged-merchandise-body in that funhouse charity mirror in my underwear, spring stripped the house of its sheet and the sound it made matched exactly the sound the tables made in that other schoolroom, where they did it to us, where they would drag the metal-legged tables scraping across the cement floor into position for the doing of it, and with that grinding rumble I was down on the floor in a fetal crouch, screaming, *No! No more!* like it was all happening again.

'Shhhh,' I said out loud to my screeching chest down there in my crouch. 'It was just the snow sliding off the roof,' I said, and I stroked my own cheek and put my sweat-sticky palm against my breastbone until my heartbeat soaked into my hand and memory stopped traveling faster than sound, until *History* passed and *Now* caught up with me again.

I was determined to go through with this.

I stood up. But don't think for a minute that I just looked at myself in that mirror wearing nothing but my underwear.

I'd taken off my shoes but I still had some teenager's socks on, bulky white ones with floppy elastic. I'm only twenty-six, whatever the hell that means. And what I stared at in front of that mirror were those gray-white socks I'd salvaged from some generous matron's contribution. I don't think she'd even washed them before dumping them into the big black plastic trash bag I pulled them out of. Perfect victim socks.

From down there by the drooping socks, my eyes jumped all the way up to the face in the mirror, by-passing whatever lay between ankles and eye-brows – my eyes didn't even strafe that terrain, the scene of the crimes.

It looked familiar, the mirror face. Not inhuman at all. She would probably even be called pretty, with her long, thin nose. Okay, it has a bump in the middle, but not the kind of bump that pokes forward like a parrot beak. It's the Slavic kind that flattens for half a centimeter, jutting a bit to each side, then continues on its way again, all straight and narrow and fine. A nose with character. My uncle's nose, my mother's brother, the dandy, the lady's man, who used to flirt with me when I was ten and make me feel special.

And the lips too were just like before – thin, but not pursed, not like they'd really be full if only her face would relax; they simply were that way. Thin. Elegant. And her fingers, I noticed when I reached up to take the clip out of my hair, they were long and elegant too. A pianist's fingers. You'd never guess from looking at them what else they'd done, touched.

When I'd unclipped my dingy hair and it fell onto my shoulders it had the audacity to swing, like those slow-motion ads for shampoo, heavy and lush, at least where the ends weren't split since I haven't done much with it, hardly even trimmed it, since before.

I still couldn't bring myself to look below the neck; I kept staring into those mirror eyes in order not to. And those eyes, the damned deceivers, looked . . . How can I say it? *Normal.* Or nearly. They reminded me of the sky while they kept us there. Not because my eyes are blue – they're brown, like my hair – but because you couldn't tell a thing from them. I remember my shock back then that the sun just kept on shining. The sky ought to have bled. The clouds should have dripped down the horizon like clots.

And then I thought, well, maybe my body won't betray me. So, finally, I looked.

I took in the whole of her, in one quick glance – breasts, belly, thighs. Crotch.

And do you know what I saw? I saw a young woman's body.

Oh sure, there were those crepey stretchmarks just above her panty line, from that pregnancy. But that's not exactly blue numbers, now, is it?

What stood in the mirror was a plain, ordinary, slim, *unmarked* young woman's body.

I had nothing. Nothing at all to show for it.

That's when I got the idea, standing there in front of that mirror. I didn't do it, but I considered it, quite seriously. I can still imagine it, step-by-step, my own private blood feud:

I'd go to the desk where we keep our supplies.

I can see myself getting out the exacto knife and breaking off the chipped tip so the razor edge is fresh. Back at the mirror, I would pull one of the breasts up out of the bra cup and, with the blade, scratch a circle around the dark brown of the nipple. I imagine if it draws blood it'll leave a scar, so I'd wait to see if blood surfaces. At first, I can't picture blood coming, so I imagine cutting the circle again, only harder. And again, till scarlet-black rivulets come trickling down the breast, and that's how I'd know how deep to make the other cuts. Then I'd slice the other nipple the same way. Then, I carve a graceful red line around the belly reflected in that mirror, framing all the stretchmarks. And from the bottom of that circle I cut an arrow down to the pubic hair. Neatly. I wouldn't slash her face, and certainly not her wrists or throat – no way I'd finish the job for them. But I would carve four more arrows – two inside each thigh: one marking the traffic to her asshole, the other pointing cuntward.

It wouldn't hurt. Well, maybe later it would. But not right then. Right then, it would feel refreshing. Hot at first, and as the air hit the droplets, tingly. Alive.

I'd stand there in front of the mirror for a long time watching the red stains soak into the underwear, looking like a gory porno poster.

A body weeping blood from every pore.

'This is good,' I would decree, out loud. Like God.

Part Two

I
CARE

Logical Consequences

Almost five and small for his age, Zero stands in the paneled hallway, the windowless dark wood corridor lined with the doors – to all the bedrooms, the study, the bathrooms, the library. His back to the wall, he listens. From behind the closed door of the study come the voices of the man he has been told to call 'Babbo' – because that's what little Italian children call their daddy, almost like 'Babo' like the kids say back home – and the woman he calls 'Mamma', though she isn't and he knows it and she knows it, too. 'Babbo' and 'Mamma' speak softly, seriously. 'Mamma' cries but 'Babbo' sounds business-like, like when he 'negotiates' with Zero – only they always call him 'Enzo' – about just how 'Babbo' will hurt him the next time 'Enzo' pees the bed, or poops it, like he's pretending he's talking to a grown-up. But grown-ups don't poop or pee their bed and everybody knows that too.

Only 'Enzo' can get 'Mamma' to stop crying, as everybody knows. He just does one of his imitations of a cowboy getting shot, just jumps into the air and kicks his feet way out and falls so it looks like he's landed flat on his back, but he knows how to catch himself a little here and a little there so it doesn't hurt. 'Mamma' cries out like a scared kid, 'Oh, you'll hurt yourself, Enzo, oh!' But she's laughing too and claps her hands and giggles. Sometimes he can even get 'Babbo' to laugh; sometimes.

He has his cap pistol he's had always, from before, with the white handle, though some of the plastic on one side of the handle has cracked off so he got the tape out from 'Babbo's' desk one day. He sneaked into that room where he's not allowed to be, ever, never, never, and went through all the drawers until he found the tape so he could wrap it around and around the handle and make sure he didn't lose any more of its whiteness. He found other things in the drawers: something like a knife in a squared-off leather sheath he'd seen 'Babbo' open letters with, he wanted to take that but left it for later; and he left a picture of what looked like 'Mamma' a long time ago only she had a fat belly and she was smiling, wearing a straw hat and holding up knitting needles with a pink knitted thing hanging down.

Way at the back of the long top drawer, he found a little stack of photo slides kept together with a rubber band. He held the slides up to the window light and saw that each one showed a different naked lady; one of them was holding a heart-shaped piece of paper that looked like some kid had colored it red, holding it right in front of her peepee but her boobies were hanging down and she was smiling.

Another lady was on her hands and knees and had her po-po looking right at you and she was smiling at you too. And there were others. All these he took. He put the rubber band back around them and put them in his pocket and later he put them in that place he found in the cellar where he could get to if he was very careful to wait till he knew for sure the big fat *portiere* was upstairs having his lunch. Then he could get to a wooden box that was all sooty and empty and old; he kept his Amaretto cookie tin in there, with other things too, like the piece of white plastic that cracked off of his pistol handle, and like the first caps he used up when 'Babbo' and 'Mamma' took him from Her; She bought him those caps.

Now he waited outside the closed door to hear what 'Babbo' said to 'Mamma' and he tried to get the words to come out right but some of them he didn't know in this funny language they talked to him in and he talked back in – not real words at all, dumb fake words for things that had whole other names, just like he did, whose name was really Zero and everybody knew it but they all pretended it was 'Enzo'.

'Babbo' lectured to 'Mamma', 'Discipline . . .' Zero heard him say, and '. . . History.' Then he said, '. . . a monster on our hands,' and Zero pictured the monster, with sharp green scales, and bloody teeth. 'Babbo' kept talking. 'You must understand this, Mariella . . . our responsibility.' And then he shouted, 'WAR!'

'Mamma' must have said something into her hands because Zero couldn't make out any of her words at all, just a sound like she was almost choking.

'Babbo' must have moved nearer the door, because suddenly Zero could hear everything he said. 'You don't have to do it. I will. But we must present a united front. If you do not respect my authority how do you expect the boy to learn to do so?'

From the muffled rustlings, Zero could tell that they were about to come out of the room so he ran quickly into the bathroom and was just closing the door when a hand stopped the action. It was 'Babbo'. The man craned his head around to look sternly down into the child's blinking eyes, there behind the door.

'Enzo, please come with me.'

Zero slid his spine down along the wall and crouched in a ball on the floor, slipping the fingers of his left hand under the door and holding on tightly. He was mute.

'Enzo, please don't make Babbo use force. I am going to your room and I expect you to meet me there.' He walked away.

Zero didn't move. He hardly breathed. He waited. 'Babbo' must have been waiting too. There was nothing happening for a long time. Then, just as Zero began to loosen his grip on the underside of the door someone came into the bathroom so quietly he didn't hear it, but as soon as he sensed the presence of someone standing in front of him Zero kicked out with both his legs. His back slid farther down the wall so that he lay flat now, on the cold ceramic tiles, and flailed his little legs and kicked his hard-heeled shoes at the naked shins in front of him which, he now saw, and to his regret, belonged not to 'Babbo' but to 'Mamma.' There she stood, being careful not to cry out in pain and give him away, whispering just loudly enough to get past the grunts of his attack. 'Go in to him,' she begged. 'Please, Enzo, he'll only come and drag you in there, my little treasure, let him do what he wants, please, we can't win.' The crease between her eyebrows seemed a gash he could have fallen into.

She reached out her hand to him. He took it. He stood and for a short moment with her arms on his narrow back, and with his face resting against her – he was taller than before so his face reached now above her waist, though still below her soft breasts.

Slowly, she led him, his arms tight around her hips, into the bedroom they said was his. Prying his hands loose, 'Mamma' hesitantly, obediently, surrendered him into the grip of her husband. She left the room; where she went and what she did then, while it was going on, Zero would never know.

'I want to explain what I am about to do,' 'Babbo' began in the same measured adult tone he had used a few moments ago when speaking to 'Mamma,' 'because I want you to understand this is not to . . .' (here he used a word Zero didn't understand) '. . . you, but to encourage you to act in your own best interest. I am now going to place you in a diaper, complete with diaper pins and rubber pants, and then into your pajamas. We shall treat you the way you behave, like the baby you pretend to be. You have the power here: when you have woken up several days in a row with your diaper dry and unsoiled, you won't have to wear one any more. Do you understand? Please remove your pants and underwear.'

All this time, Zero had his hand around his cap pistol's handle, deep in his pocket. But now he drew his gun.

'Don't be silly, Enzo. Put that away and do as I told you to.'

Zero aimed his pistol straight between the man's glaring eyes. Then 'POW! POW! POW! POW!' exploded from his mouth, and showed no sign of ever stopping.

'Babbo's' strong hand wrapped itself around the boy's fist and the boy's weapon, and began twisting. Zero screamed, loud, high-pitched screams, with all the force and fury he knew and didn't know. He screamed and screamed, long and loud, as 'Babbo' wrenched from his grasp the toy cap gun with the broken and mended white plastic handle. And as Zero stood there on the deep-tufted dark-blue, shag rug, shrieking and howling, unremittingly, he urinated – in a stream too gushing to be absorbed by the denim of his trousers so that it ran down his legs into a puddle around his feet, turning the carpet fibers to a dirty black. 'Babbo' dropped the gun onto the rug and, holding the dripping child at arm's length, well away from him, his face twisted in fury and revulsion, carried 'Enzo' into the bathroom where he seemed on the verge of throwing the little boy into the empty tub. But 'Babbo' braked at the last moment and placed the child, though not gently, into the wide white bathtub. 'Wash yourself, young man,' he seethed. 'Get hold of yourself. You hear me?' Then he left the room.

Zero listened a moment to how many heavy steps the man was taking down the long corridor. When he was sure that 'Babbo' had gone all the way down the hall, into *lo studio* and not into 'Enzo's' room, Zero scrambled as quietly as he could out of the tub. He ran into the bedroom and reclaimed his gun from the dampness of the rug. Once back in the bathroom, he closed the door slowly, and, by pushing the handle down in advance, made the closure as noiseless as possible. Then he began peeling off his damp and chilling pants, one-handedly so as not to loosen his grip on his dear pistol.

God Bless the Child

Mette smelled the envelope, the onionskin kind designed for flight and slashed around its edges with red and blue and white diagonals. That acrid odor of garlic seeming to arise from it turned out, however, to emanate from her own fingers; she'd been unpacking groceries when the mail was delivered. 'Zheljka Nadarević' read the baroque handwriting. Originally addressed via a United Nations refugee agency and with a Rome postmark, the letter had been forwarded once within Italy, several times inside Norway, and finally to Mette – or rather, care of Hans Olav Kaldstad. Only bureaucratic missives had arrived in the mail for the Nadarević couple these last months, letters from someone at the Immigration Department named Heyerdal Ruud, postcards from the refugee placement people about language classes for immigrants or free medical clinic appointments; guests in Norway got good service, it seemed. No hand-addressed or foreign envelopes for either Mesud or Zheljka had ever before been found in the green metal postbox outside the Kaldstads' big front door.

At first, Mette put the letter atop the pile of mail which awaited Hans Olav's attention in the hall and returned to putting away her Monday morning food purchases. But then, leaving the freezer door wide open, she re-entered the hall to have another look.

The original address had flowed from some fountain pen filled with sober dark-blue ink. The forwarding addresses, however, were pre-printed labels, routing it along the bureaucratic highway. Until the last one, that is. Someone had etched the Kaldstads' address into the only remaining space using a splotching ballpoint pen so scratchy that it had ripped tiny holes in the bulky envelope.

There was no room for yet another forwarding address. Mette rummaged among the used stationery she saved in her desk for an envelope good enough to forward the letter in one last time. Cringing at the specter of a letter from her arriving at Zheljka's mailbox wearing a shabby envelope, Mette closed the desk drawer and, on the shopping list affixed to the side of the refrigerator by a metal magnet resembling a little owl, she penciled child-like block letters: 'Envelope, C3' and then appended, '– white.'

Where to put the letter in the meantime? Yes, she slid it into her purse so that once she had bought the new envelope, she could send it on immediately. When Mette returned to unpacking her groceries, the red light on the still-open freezer door blinked a warning.

*　　*　　*

Later that evening, while Hans Olav watched the news, Mette carried her purse to their bedroom and took the letter out. What could it be? Coming from Italy, from a Dottore LoSchiavo it could be about Zero. She dismissed that thought as silly: Zheljka had lived in Rome long enough that it might just as well be from some long-lost friend. The handwriting, seemed manly, despite its flourishes. In what language would someone from Italy communicate with Zheljka?

As the letter was marked *Urgente*, Mette resolved to go the very next day to buy the envelope. In fact, the whole thing slipped her mind until Wednesday evening when, while searching for her reading glasses in the inner sanctum of her purse, those red, blue and white airmail slashes caught her eye. At that, some metallic-tasting chemical hit her bloodstream, fluttering her heart. *Urgente*. She'd better leave the letter propped in front of the side door, the one leading to the carport, so she couldn't possibly exit the following day without stepping on it. But then Hans Olav would see it too, and notice how long ago it had been forwarded last and then she'd either have to make up some excuse or face his chastising her for being, yet again, irresponsible.

Mette placed the letter in her underwear drawer, at the front, where she couldn't help but see it.

And she did see it too, early on Thursday morning. She read its travel history once again, tracing the

147

path it had followed to her hands. To *her* hands, it had arrived. Wasn't there meaning in that? Let's say it was about Zero; wouldn't it be better if *she* were the one to face facts first? Then she could warn Zheljka, soften the impact? After all, any news, good or bad, would be a blow to a mother who'd given her own child away. It would be a kindness to Zheljka for Mette to open the letter.

But there were, as always, Hans Olav's moral principles to contend with, his sermons on 'private property' and 'respect'. On such issues, among others, he was scrupulous: if, for example, she wanted her glasses and they were in her purse upstairs, he'd bring down the whole bag; Hans Olav's hand had never once entered her purse without her consent. Of course, Mette knew that also worked to her advantage, given the strange habit she had of taking things home unpaid for. She could hide them, secure in the knowledge that Hans Olav would never even open her drawers, much less ransack them. But, no, Hans Olav would not approve of her reading other people's mail, even as an act of kindness. And Mette herself wondered if her motives were, in fact, pure.

Thus, too confused to think things through, Mette replaced the letter in her dresser drawer and decided to decide later.

After the weekend, when Mette finally did open the letter to Zheljka, seated at the kitchen table late enough on Monday morning to be sure Hans Olav was gone for the day, she did so carefully, using an exacto knife to take but a thin slice off the upper envelope edge – just in case she wanted to tape it shut later. After all those forwardings, who could tell at what point the envelope had been opened accidentally?

Inside were two separate documents: one, a handwritten letter penned in Italian, in the same fluid and ornate script as the original address on the envelope; the other, a typed text, turned out to be the translation of that letter into English.

Dear Signora Nadarević,

As I am sure you already have ascertained from both the envelope and my letterhead, my wife and I are those into whose keeping you delivered your son . . .

'I knew it!' Mette shouted.

We have, by the way, rechristened him 'Enzo' in our Catholic church. That name, we determined, approximates the sound of 'Zero' but does not elicit the endless inquiries, and even ridicule, which his birth name, in our society, would certainly have occasioned.

If you are now reading these words, it will be thanks to the efficiency of the United Nations Refugee Commissariat which has agreed, first, to furnish this translation (I must compose so important a missive in my own language), and, second, to make sure the letter is forwarded, assuming, of course, that they are able to locate you, and that you have continued to use the name by which we knew you. They have been paragons of discretion, informing me neither as to your whereabouts nor even as to their success or failure in locating you. This, despite how frustrating that may have been for me, and, I might add, how detrimental any delay might prove to the future well-being of little Enzo. My contact with you must therefore be at best indirect, at worst uncertain or impossible. Or too late.

Damn! The phone was ringing. Was it too late? Was the boy dying? As she ran from the kitchen to the living room extension she flipped to the end of the translation:

I apologize deeply for our failure adequately to discharge the responsibility with which you so un-selfishly entrusted us, and remain,

> *Your humble servant,*
> *Dott. Pietro LoSchiavo*

Oh God, no! Attempting to scan the letter for words like *death* or *accident*, Mette shouldered the receiver: 'Hello, this is Mette Kaldstad.' She'd never questioned this Norwegian etiquette of answering a phone by stating one's name until Zheljka had complained, 'What right does the caller have to be told who is here?'

It was Hans Olav's voice which entered her

ear. He wanted her to find something in his study; she had no choice but to put the crinkling pages down next to the phone and stand up. Only then did she notice that her legs could barely support her.

She did as asked: she read out the insurance information her husband required and then would have hung up, but he said, 'Mette, what's up?'

How could he always tell?

'Nothing, I'm just . . .' What should she say? 'I'm just reading an article that upsets me.'

'What about?'

'About . . . children. In Brazil. Being stolen and killed and their organs sold.'

'Mette, there's nothing you can do about it.'

'But it happens, Hans Olav. Such things go on.'

'Try not to worry, sweetheart.'

Where had she left off reading?

. . . or too late.

Let me first allay all catastrophic anxieties the fact of this letter may already have engendered: at this writing, your son is quite alive and not ill in any life threatening way.

How considerate of this 'Dott. Pietro LoSchiavo' to know that's just what a mother would think first. Well anyway, that's just what Mette had thought. Wouldn't Zheljka have become worried? Or what if she'd felt hopeful? Maybe, Mette thought, and the idea brought an odd pleasure, maybe Zheljka *hoped* Zero was dead, beyond any need for her to take responsibility for him.

He is, however, I am sorry to inform you, not fully well. And it is for this reason I am taking the extreme, and, if I may say so, painful for all concerned, action of contacting you. As you may well imagine, a great deal of deliberation has preceded my writing. Nor would I be doing so now did I not consider it to be in the child's best interest.

If I am to give a thorough understanding of the predicament in which we find ourselves, I cannot help but broach those personal historical topics to which you so . . .

The bloody phone was ringing again. Running to answer it, Mette thought how good it was that she, Mette, had opened someone else's mail: Zero was in trouble and Zheljka didn't want him. Maybe the children in Brazil weren't even kidnapped; maybe they were sold.

'Hello, this is Mette Kaldstad.'

'We're calling from the Heart and Lung Association, Mrs Kaldsen. Thank you for supporting us during our last . . .'

'Our name is Kald*stad*, not Kald*sen*. My husband takes care of our charity donations and he's not home. Excuse me, you see, I'm right in the middle of doing something . . .' From now on, if the phone rang again she would let the machine get it – if, that

is, her curiosity could endure those six rings before
it took over.

*. . . I cannot help but broach those personal historical
topics to which you so strenuously resisted being
made privy during the negotiations regarding our
adoption of the boy. Without making this information
explicit, no appropriate disposition of this matter
can possibly be determined. If I am mistaken in that
assumption, I pray for your understanding and
forgiveness.*

*During the first fifteen years of our marriage, my
wife Mariella, was the unfortunate victim of an
inability to carry a child to term . . .*

Mette's and Hans Olav's was also a fifteen-year
childless marriage. The feeling of destiny being at
work gave Mette the chills: this letter seemed *meant*
for her.

*While the majority of her nearly annual miscarriages
occurred relatively early, that is, during the first
trimester, three of them came well into the pregnancy,
forcing her to undergo long and difficult labors . . .*

'I've never even conceived,' Mette whispered.

*. . . only to deliver well-developed infants, already
deceased. There was no way our religious convictions
would allow us to protect her from these recurring
and deeply disturbing losses. The final stillbirth*

153

occasioned so severe an emotional response in my wife that she, I am sorry to admit, attempted to take her own life, and by means which resulted not in her death but in her irreversible sterility. For many months after, she refused even to speak. Her physician and I determined that, were she to return to good health, her childlessness must of necessity be remediated. It was at that point that her doctor and I began our search for a child to adopt.

She was lucky, Mette thought, this, what's her name? Mariella. Her husband understood her: Hans Olav had never wanted to adopt.

Notwithstanding that our financial capacity to care for a child was, and continues to be, excellent, and that our moral fitness must be considered beyond reproach, we understood that the established agencies for adoption would not be an option open to us, given Mariella's age, condition and history of instability.

Through connections which I have by virtue of my position in the government, we were able to forge a link with the less conventional channels for locating available children. I intentionally requested an older child to avoid the 'Russian Roulette' of receiving an infant who has yet to demonstrate its capacity to survive. There was no worse fate I could imagine for my wife than to lose to death also an adopted baby! I am sure you understand this as I imagine you to be one forced by the will of God to know and endure great loss.

Yes, I am, Mette thought, moved by his appreciation – until she remembered this letter wasn't to her.

In fact, your bravery and self-sacrifice in relinquishing your child to assure him a better life are capacities for which, Signora, I hold you in the highest esteem, as a paragon of the meaning of the word 'mother'. And it is in my trust for your continued ability to choose another's welfare over your own that I am so presumptuous as to contact you now.

This was just a little too much for Mette to swallow. When someone gives a child away, she gives away her right to the title 'mother' and must renounce her claims to maternal dignity, to the authority, the privileges, the luxuries, such as looking in the mirror and knowing that you too have fulfilled your destiny, have succeeded as a woman, have contributed to the future of the world. Mette's eyes filled with tears. Did Zheljka know what she had done?

I can see now that any experienced parent would ridicule what may only be seen as our naïveté in assuming that so fragile a soul as my wife could meet the challenge of an, as it turns out, equally fragile adopted war-child. I must, I am afraid, admit that Mariella has not proven herself up to the task, although not, you understand, through any fault of her own: I forgive her for her incapacity. From the start, the child was terribly difficult, and would have

155

seemed so to any woman, even one in the most robust of mental conditions. Nor have I been able to lighten the burden; Enzo's care has fallen primarily to my wife as my work is highly demanding and leaves me little time for domestic pursuits.

'Domestic pursuits! He sounds just like Hans Olav.'

The problems which Enzo exhibits were nascent upon his arrival and have only worsened and become entrenched during his time with us. From the very beginning, he has wet his bed at night. All our efforts and strategies to cure or even ameliorate this habit have failed dismally. And we have certainly tried!

Mariella attempted an elaborate bedtime ritual of storytelling and lullabies, until I ordered her to stop rewarding him for his bad behavior. Once she had ceased, his symptoms proved not only not to have been relieved, but also to have been exacerbated.

We tried punishment, attempting, for example, to shame him by insisting he wear diapers, against which he put forth an aggressive resistance. I bought him small devices: a buzzer for his bed which is triggered by wetness, an instrument which delivers an electric shock each time he urinates, and so forth. Nothing at all has worked.

Not even corporal punishment, of whatever severity, has seemed to make an impact on his incontinence.

Obviously, we have had him examined medically

but his lack of control is decidedly not physical. Not only has he not stopped wetting his bed, but recently, Signora Nadarević, and it pains me greatly to have to tell you this, he has, upon occasion, soiled it as well. You begin to see our dilemma.

I believe, however, the behaviours which have caused Mariella's condition to deteriorate so dramatically are the rages and tantrums Enzo directs specifically at her. He screams at her, for example: 'You're not my real mother, you're my fake mother! I hate you!' Repeating the phrase, 'I hate you,' endlessly, and in sing-song. He also refuses to relinquish the white-handled cap pistol he was carrying the day we received him from you; he threatens my wife with it, and, as ludicrous as it may sound given his size and age, he actually does frighten her.

Please understand that I am quite fond of Enzo; I imagine that my expressing the difficulties we are experiencing so emphatically may obscure that fact. The moments when he is peaceful, he is a kind and tender little fellow. And he is capable of great humor: he acts out elaborate cowboy-and-Indian scenes in which he plays all the parts, changing his voice and disguising his accent, dropping on the spot as if dead. He is also very bright, and unexpectedly adaptable. He has learned to speak Italian in record time, for which his kindergarten teacher commends him. She does complain, however, that Enzo is unwilling to participate in organized activities of any kind and appears incapable of establishing friendships with the other children.

We must admit we are daunted by his willfulness –
a trait which would profit him were it directed toward
the good. Such tenacity in the service of negativity
and rebellion, however, accomplishes naught but to
alienate even those who would wish him well.

Nonetheless, I believe that the problems to which I
refer here, though terribly challenging, would have
proved manageable were it not for the response they
provoke in my wife. She is cowed by Enzo, is un-
healthily in his sway; she spoils him and thus can
carry through no predetermined course of discipline.
In fact, she attempts, covertly, to sabotage all efforts I
exert to compensate for her default.

Most recently she has returned to being mute – with
everyone, that is, except the child. She has ceased
to dress herself and refuses to leave the house. Our
physician has diagnosed her malady as 'major
depression'. I am most concerned she might revert
to her suicidal behaviour, which certainly would
serve no one – not her, not me, and obviously not
Enzo.

Mette at her kitchen table felt she knew what was
coming next, smiled, at first covertly and then
broadly.

I presume you can understand the difficult and
inevitable conclusion at which I have arrived: I no
longer believe that we can provide the child with a
good home.

'But I can!' Mette held the letter in front of her in both hands and spoke to it, as if to a person. Hardly bothering to contain her joy, Mette ran up the stairs to her bedroom clutching the letter to her breast like a flat baby.

From the bottom drawer of her magical dresser she took out a packet wrapped in tissue paper containing a baby's sweater which she had knitted in pink. Of course, it had never occurred to her that she might get an older child. Or a boy.

She unwrapped the treasure and inhaled its scent, though it bore none of the sweet aroma of an infant. She curled up on the spread of her carefully made bed, pressing the sweater to her chest with one hand and holding the letter with the other. 'I'll take him, Dottore LoSchiavo,' she declared, using her forearm, not the sweater, to wipe the tears from her smiling cheeks.

I am writing to you in the hope that your life circumstances have stabilized in such a way that you might deem it in Enzo's best interest for him to return to you.

Failing that, I am having prepared a list of suitable placements for Enzo here in Italy.

Mette sat up abruptly. 'Placements?' What did that mean?

You understand now, too, my frustration over the delay caused by my not being able to contact you directly. I could have telephoned and saved time, a commodity in short supply in this situation: I have determined to wait until just after Easter, two months from the date on this letter, for a response from you. If by that time I have not heard from you at either number on my letterhead, or at the above address, I will place Enzo in foster care or an institution.

The date! Easter was a week ago. Was she too late?

Her eyes searched the letterhead for the phone number, but she restrained herself; she ought to finish reading the letter first.

I will arrange to do so 'blind', that is, without our being informed of his whereabouts. I do so both to avoid argument between me and my wife and to protect us against any unhealthy impulse to waver in our resolve and thereby occasion yet another destabilizing displacement of the boy.

As I am not a person for whom such expressions come easily, I beg you to infer the immense grief this decision causes me. I will miss little Enzo. He was, as I am all too well aware, the only opportunity Our Lord is likely ever to grant me of experiencing being a father.

I apologize deeply for our failure adequately to discharge the responsibility with which you so unselfishly entrusted us, and remain,
Your humble servant,
Dott. Pietro LoSchiavo

Now Mette grabbed up the phone and dialed the operator. 'Can you tell me the area code for Italy – Rome, Italy?'

She pressed each button carefully: double zero for an international line, thirty-nine for Italy, zero-six for Rome. And then the number. But as a foreign ringing began at the other end, Mette slammed down the receiver. What time was it in Rome? She called the operator again to check if Rome and Oslo share the same time zone. They do. So she'd have to wait till this evening.

But what if it was his *office* phone number printed on the stationery? Lying on her bed, the letter at her breast, Mette imagined Dottore Pietro LoSchiavo behind a glossy, ornately carved mahogany desk, the kind of antique whose inlaid green leather blotter had a thin red line tooled around its perimeter. On the desk, an elegant fountain pen filled with deep-blue ink lay waiting. Dottore's stylish secretary would buzz him from the outer office to announce an incoming call . . . But then, not recognizing the caller's name, he would instruct her to take a message and not to disturb him further.

She'd have to pretend to be some kind of official. That would get her through. Mrs Kaldstad from – what had he called it in his letter? From the United Nations Refugee Commissariat of Norway.

Mette sat up and placed the letter carefully on her lap and the tiny sweater, open-armed, beside her on the bed. She preened her hair and smoothed her skirt, modeling her comportment on that of a female

161

bureaucrat she'd seen on TV the previous evening, the official in charge of some welfare service under attack for providing too little to one sector of victims and too much to another. The woman had seemed virtually invulnerable.

Again, Mette pressed the phone number's digits slowly.

'*Buongiorno.*' It was a *woman's* voice!

'Long-distance calling for Pietro LoSchiavo,' Mette said in English. But she had apparently pronounced the name incorrectly. '*Lo-Zhavo*', she had said, like the '*Zh*' in the English word 'treasure', like the '*Zh*' at the beginning of the name *Zheljka*.

'Loh-skee-AHH-voh,' the woman mouthed back distinctly. 'Doh-TAW-ray Lo-Skee-AHH-voh is not here. May I take a message, please?'

'Is there another number where he can be reached?'

'Yes, signora, at his office.'

Mette strained to hear if a child's voice was among the background noises. Should she mention Zero, or rather – what was it they'd renamed him? – *Enzo*?

'Wait,' Mette said, 'I have to get something to write with . . .' But regretted the words the moment they were out of her mouth: long-distance operators always have a pen. And indeed, it seemed to have awakened suspicion.

'Who did you say is calling, please?' the woman inquired.

Mette hung up.

*　　*　　*

As her heart rate slowed and her sweaty palms dried, Mette flopped back onto the bed and began to cry. She was about to lose Zero. She couldn't phone the *dottore*, and mailing him a letter would take too long.

But wait! Wasn't there also a fax number printed on the letterhead? She sat up and looked. And there it was! This would surely be at his work, not his house. She'd fax him. She could send it from the post office. She'd never done that before, but they'd know how.

Only, if she sent a fax, she'd need official stationery . . .

Then it came to her: she wouldn't pretend to be from the UN, she would just be herself, Mette Kaldstad. She would tell Dottore, in English, that she had hosted Zheljka and Mesud when they arrived in Norway and that now, because their refugee status was so delicate, Zheljka had asked Mette to handle all the arrangements for her. She wanted Zero back – or 'Enzo' – so would Dottore please phone immediately – or rather, sometime when Hans Olav wouldn't be home.

Suddenly Mette had to pee. She folded the letter-head page of Dottore's letter and slipped it into her bra as she made her way, knees trembling, toward the gleaming white marble bathroom. In the wall of mirrors over the sinks she saw the rosiness of her cheeks, the glow in her eyes. Someone once had referred to her as 'motherly' and Mette hadn't understood why. Now she did: she did look 'motherly', even if more suited, chronologically, to looking grandmotherly. Her eyebrows raised, her forehead smoothed, her stature increased, and Mette addressed her own image tenderly: 'I'm going to have a child!' she crooned.

Mette's breast had warmed the letterhead page when she removed it from her brassière. She found a pen, noted the fax number on a slip of paper and then slid the note carefully into her wallet, behind the photograph of her parents when they were young and had just arrived in Norway, the picture in which she was just an infant bundled in her mother's arms.

She returned the rest of the letter and its translation to their neatly sliced envelope. From her underwear drawer, Mette took out the bundle she'd made of Zheljka's shawl. Untying the fringes scrupulously so they wouldn't tangle, Mette placed the letter such that it served as a platform upon which to stack the coins – the seventeen twenty-kroner pieces – and Zheljka's passport. She retied first two opposing corners of the shawl, and then the remaining two. Mette hugged the bundle to her breast and kissed it lightly. Then she replaced it in the dresser drawer, all the way at the back.

Standing graciously before her closet door, Mette picked out what to wear to the post office.

Send-Off

The newspaper image of a tattered corpse rested on the retina of Pietro LoSchiavo's mind's eye; another player in the Italian mafia-government cat-and-mouse game – this time, a Calabrian judge – had met his untimely, though not unforeseen, end while shutting the *portone* of his State-guarded apartment complex. The picture seemed to Pietro an object lesson about the narrow though familiar path one must tread between honor on the one hand and pragmatism on the other. Pietro, as so many of his countrymen, regarded himself as an expert at negotiating such predictable public chaos.

But this business with Enzo was something other. This insinuated itself beneath the skin of his private sphere, wherein Pietro considered the soul of Italian order to reside. All this *private* messiness – their failed fertility, Mariella's failed psyche, this failed adoption – constituted dishonor at the core: within the family.

And so Pietro would deliver Enzo to Sweden. He would not fly to Norway, the child's ultimate destination, because both the Swedes and the Italians, unlike the Norwegians, had elected to join the European Union within which Pietro, child in hand, could now travel without once being stopped for passport control. As the borders within Scandinavia were likewise open for those countries' citizens, the Kaldstad woman could drive Enzo across into Norway similarly unchecked. Thus, by arriving in Göteborg, they dodged all risk of border officials apprehending either of them at this not-quite-legal exportation of human life. Nor would Pietro's passport bear the stamp of his disgrace.

Pietro argued with himself that no one could have been expected to succeed at such an adoption. This 'Enzo'. A war-baby. A helpless, furious, incontinent victim. It is not easy to save someone's life. It had been all he could do to save his wife; who could blame him for not managing to wrest this unfortunate child from the dripping teeth of history?

Pietro, having carefully assessed what might promote the smoothest transition, had waited until that very morning to tell Enzo of his impending departure. Would it help the boy to be told he was going back to his mother? How much resentment he bore her, no one knew. Would it be easier if he believed he was being sent to another family? Pietro couldn't measure to which extent the boy had developed an attachment to him and his wife in the time, now nine months, that he had lived as their son. In the event that the bond between the child and Mariella proved intense, and in order to avoid his wife's intervening, Pietro had arranged to fly the child to Sweden without her knowledge. He had sent her to visit her sister, Maria Grazia, in Perugia; she would be presented upon her return with the irreversible fact of Enzo's absence. Thus Pietro could spare the boy any potentially traumatizing confrontations.

And he would be saving Mariella the internal anguish which he alone, as a man, would now face: making the decision; negotiating its implicit moral ambiguities; tolerating the brutality of the actual moment of separation; and then, living on, bearing alone the inevitable grate and nag of conscience. Only he, Pietro, would be subjected to whatever violent, or indifferent, response might come from the boy. Why should fragile Mariella have to endure that punishment? He was robust. He could face it.

Pietro made them breakfast. Tuesday was the maid's day off and that was part of the plan. Silvana was their housekeeper; she'd served the LoSchiavo family since Pietro himself was a boy and always had her Tuesdays free. She and her employer had agreed that, being absent on that day, she need never admit to Mariella her complicity in the scheme. She'd never liked Enzo, anyway.

As Enzo kneeled on a chair at the white enameled kitchen table, dipping his breakfast cornetto into lukewarm, weak and sweetened coffee-milk, Pietro himself packed the boy's belongings. The man folded and folded, placing one carefully ironed piece of apparel neatly atop the other. For the boy's flight, he selected a brand-new pair of spring trousers with matching crew-neck sweater, polished loafers and even a little cap. Scandinavia, he had read, was enduring an unseasonably cold spring and there should be no doubt that the LoSchiavo family had done its best. The rest of Enzo's effects Pietro placed into the two sports-duffels he'd purchased specifically for this day; these nylon bags folded small enough so as not to awaken Mariella's suspicions when he brought them home, and yet expanded to hold everything associated with the child. Pietro wanted nothing left behind to aggrieve the hands, eyes or heart of his wife.

'Enzo. Please come into my study for a moment.' Would the boy follow without protest? The man refused to look back, but heard Enzo walking behind him.

'Please sit down. Enzo, I must tell you that we will be leaving on a trip today, just you and I.'

'Where are we going?' Enzo asked. Then added, '"Babbo"?'

Pietro would give out information in small portions, to avoid any outbursts. 'Have you ever heard of a country named Sweden? Yes? That's where we're going. Way up north, near where *Babbo Natale* lives.'

'But Christmas was a long time ago.' As he spoke, Enzo flipped the lid of the desk's sunken brass inkwell open and closed, and open and closed. 'Is Mamma coming too? Why are we going?'

Pietro smiled. 'Please leave that alone. Go get dressed and I'll tell you more as we're on our way.' Standing now, Pietro took the boy's cheeks between his palms and lowered his face, preparing to kiss his forehead. Enzo, however, jerked his head to one side, and slid away so fast that Pietro's lips caressed only empty air. He sank down in the chair Enzo had just left and put his own head between his palms, massaging his temples and then rubbing his eyes.

When, finally, all was ready, and when the boy and the man stood by the apartment's highly polished, solid wood door, the duffel bags lined up beside one another, and after Pietro had taken their similar beige raincoats from the hall closet and helped Enzo solicitously into his, one arm at a time, and stooped to button each of the small buttons, then Pietro squatted down in order to look into the boy's eyes, deeper and longer than ever before. It was then he heard himself inquire, most respectfully, 'Do you have your pistol with you?'

Enzo smiled broadly, hiking up his coat to reach his pants pocket, from which he withdrew the gun, displaying proudly first its right side then its left. For some reason – Pietro found it absolutely unaccountable – the boy chose that moment, gun in hand, to put his arms around the man's neck and kiss his cheek.

Pietro grabbed the little body to his chest, but so clumsily that Enzo cried out, 'You're hurting me!' and struggled out of the embrace.

Pietro locked the door behind them.

The boy became very excited at take-off. He asked about the noises, about the pilot, asked if the plane carried bombs, if Babbo had ever been a pilot, if there were other planes flying near them. He leaned forward, turned around in his seat, wanted to stand on his seat, wanted to kneel toward the window. When at last the seatbelt light was turned off, he began such an enthusiastic exploration of the contents of the deep pocket of the seat in front of him that the passenger in the next row turned and requested of Pietro, irritably, that he make the child stop kicking him.

It wasn't until the lunches were served that Pietro found it opportune to dispense the next bit of information: 'Enzo,' he said between bites, cheerfully, matter-of-factly, 'you'll be traveling farther than even I will today! You know that? When we get to Sweden, there will be a woman there to meet you. Her name is Mette. And you'll be going with her to even *another* country. To Norway. Did you ever hear of it? That's *really* where Babbo Natale lives, and his reindeer. So you'll be in three countries in one day: Italy, Sweden, and Norway which is right next door to Sweden.'

Enzo chewed and chewed, looking at his tray, saying nothing. Then he said, 'I have a bomber picture at school I painted with BIG wings, bigger wings than even this whole plane.'

Pietro sighed in relief: there was not to be a scene. He was handling this correctly, letting the message sink in gradually, containing the chaos.

Then, however, Enzo added, 'When we get back I'll show you.'

Pietro tested responses in his mind: *But you won't be getting back.* Or, *I'll get the picture for you and send it to you in Norway.* Maybe he should just let it slide: Enzo wasn't ready to understand. Pietro ended up saying, only, 'I'm not going to eat my piece of chocolate. Would you like to eat it, Enzo?' The child took the candy.

After the meal was cleared, Enzo played with his earphones, switching the channels as fast as the button could be pushed, changing the volume from the lowest, at which point he strained his neck forward and said, 'Louder, louder, I can't hear you!' Then he pushed the volume control button over and over until the sound must have been painfully loud and he bugged his eyes out, crying, 'Shut up! Shut up! Shut up!' And, pushing the button some more, 'There, that's better,' until once again it was too soft and he repeated his 'Louder! Louder!' chant. Over and over until he had tired of the game.

It was then that Pietro added a little information. 'You understand, Enzo? You won't be living at our house now. You'll go to a new school, too. You'll go to a Norwegian school where they speak the

Norwegian language. You understand what I'm telling you?'

Enzo flung his head away from Pietro, got on his knees and pressed his lips to the window; the vibration of the plane must have tickled them because he pulled his lips away and scraped the top lip with his bottom teeth and then his bottom lip with his top teeth, scratching and scraping. Then he put his lips back onto the window again. Finally, he turned to Pietro and said, 'I have to go make peepee.'

Good. The boy, it seemed, had decided *not* to wet his seat in protest. Pietro accompanied Enzo to the bathroom queue and asked the dignified woman at the front of it, cordially, for permission to cut in line as self-control was an issue – he began to say *for my son* but changed midway to *for the boy*.

Some time later, that same business-like woman approached Pietro's seat looking embarrassed. Into his ear she said, 'It is your little boy in the restroom, is it not? Well, he's making some odd noises in there.'

Pietro knocked. No answer. He knocked harder. 'Enzo, there are people waiting out here. Aren't you finished yet?' No response. 'Open the door, Enzo. This minute!' Nothing. 'I'm getting the stewardess to open this door, do you hear me? I'll be right back.'

There was no key for the airplane bathroom door; the flight attendant used a dinner knife to slide the latch open. Hinged at the center, the door ought to have folded inward, toward the toilet, but something blocked it. It couldn't be budged. Only when Pietro leaned his full weight against the panel marked 'Push', did the obstruction slide aside.

That obstruction was little Enzo, lying on the floor, his back jammed against the door and his foot braced against the toilet. Enzo had unrolled all the toilet paper, emptied the trash container onto the floor, smeared what must have been liquid hand soap all over the mirror. The stink of complimentary perfume rose from the stopped-up sink. Enzo lay rocking from side to side, in a puddle of his own urine.

Pietro stood over the boy. 'Enzo, get up!' he began, but the stewardess interrupted him, whispering, 'I'll see if there's a doctor on the plane. The child seems ill, don't you think?'

When Pietro put his palm to the boy's face to check for fever, Enzo winced and inhaled a sharp cry. Alone with the child in that cramped space, Pietro waited.

There was, in fact, a doctor on that plane. Enzo permitted this stranger not only to touch his face but also to hike up his sweater and place a stethoscope against his naked chest. The doctor addressed the boy gently, in what Pietro guessed to be Swedish, and then spoke to Pietro in English. 'Please ask your son – what is his name? – please ask Enzo if he is able to sit up. And would you kindly translate for us?' The doctor lifted the boy gently onto the closed toilet lid. 'Does anything hurt you?' Enzo shook his head 'no', but then his tears welled. 'Are you sure?'

Enzo's head went slowly right to left, but tears streamed. The doctor turned to Pietro, 'Do you have any dry pants the boy could put on?' Pietro hadn't thought to put extra clothes into their carry-on luggage. The stewardess managed to borrow something from the sporty, blonde mother of a wiry, freckled little boy. The mother looked at Pietro with knowing compassion as she turned over a pair of her son's satiny white boxing shorts.

'Enzo? Do you want your daddy to help you change your pants, or shall I do that?' the doctor said, looking from the boy to Pietro. Pietro translated reluctantly.

Enzo looked at the floor but pointed his finger at the doctor.

'Excuse us, please.' The toilet compartment closed and Pietro was left outside.

Enzo, the doctor told Pietro, seemed terribly disturbed, had waved a toy pistol and sobbed the same words again and again of which the doctor understood only one: *Mama*. He'd given the boy a sedative, by injection, and suggested, strongly, that Pietro have him checked at the hospital nearest the airport. He wrote out the address.

Back at their seat, Enzo soon slept. Pietro stuffed the wet trousers and underpants into two air-sickness bags, tucked the folded doctor's note into Enzo's jacket pocket, then placed the child's head on his lap. As he stroked the boy's forehead tenderly, a tear trickled down the grown man's cheek.

Pietro couldn't remember the last time he'd wept. Not even at the still-births had he cried. Now he turned his face to the window and watched the clouds. His one consolation was that he had spared his wife all of this.

Happiness

Beate, can you feel the warmth of the sun on your earth, or maybe on your stone? It's spring now. Of course, it waited till May to come, and here they call it summer. Spring up here has nothing to do with the wild flowers at home. But today, finally, at least there are baby blades of lime-green grass, whole patches, like these on your grave. We made it through the winter. Well, no, you didn't. Though maybe a death buried in darkness and snow is just a different pain than an iced-over life.

Spring scares me, Beate. Because, today, right now as I sit here, do you know what I feel? Oh this is terrible to admit:

I feel happy.

Maybe it's just a coffee jag. But I've drunk coffee every day I could get it, before, during and since the war, and not felt like this, like melting permafrost. The feeling is almost, almost, as if . . . God were good. Impossible! A God who first has me raped in hell, then, later, lifts me, happy, into the sunshine on this green *hillside? How perverse that those two things exist on one planet, in one lifetime, inside one body?*

But now, just now, it is as if there could be – *no, how?* – love. Yes. Again. In this world. Even for her.

She puckered up her lips to gather spit in her mouth, her eyes narrowing, but she paused. Her face relaxed. *Love*, she thought and shook her head.

Love.

There came a breeze. Floating clouds dimmed the sunlight and she grew afraid again. *Hope is a dangerous pastime*, she thought. *It ends in war.*

The evening before – here it was, her great confession . . .

Yesterday evening, I bought one of those drug store tests, with a little litmus stick that you pee on and it will stay beige if you're not and turn blue if you are. It turned blue. Bright, fluorescent blue.

So she wàs. Pregnant.

She said it, out loud: 'I'm pregnant, Beate, and I'm glad.'

Was there a law of nature preventing a happy pregnancy from following a horrific one, a beloved child from following an abandoned one? Was she doomed to love badly always because she had loved badly once?

Here she was, pregnant by her own husband and suddenly that seemed strange, a rare blessing. No God would let such things happen, that this baby would get to have one father while that other one had so many he had none. So who was she to thank

for this glorious day? And for the gladness at Life,
the one she was in and the one in her?

To some people, I would sound sentimental.

Now there's a joke.

I will name this baby Beate, *after you, and I will
speak Norwegian to her, the language of peace. And
when she is small I'll hold her against me without
once wishing I could vomit the very thought of her out
of me. Such luxury. To have a child you need not
hate.*

Suddenly, Zheljka felt pathetic.

And sleepy.

*Your arms, they're so grassy I could lie down in
them and you could stroke my hair. 'Hush, sweetheart, it's over now,' you could remind me. No war
has no end. No one cries for ever. I, Zheljka Gundulić
Nadarević, am alive and well and pregnant the
normal way. The sun is back. Maybe even God is
back.*

*I should freeze this moment because I know it will
pass, and who knows what else He'll shove up my
life?*

Delivery

In the men's room at the baggage-claim area of the gleaming Göteborg airport, Pietro has the drugged boy slung against his left shoulder. He threads Enzo's dangling legs awkwardly into dungarees from one of the duffels, then, with his one free hand, shoves the paper air-sickness bags containing the urine-soaked clothing into the trash can. Folding the borrowed shorts, still with one hand, he discovers the boy's pistol in its pocket. For a moment he considers heaving that too into the trash, but doesn't dare: were Enzo to awaken and discover it gone, he might create yet another scene and thus delay Pietro's departure. Pietro simply must catch that return flight. He places the pistol deep into the pocket of Enzo's dungarees.

Rolling the cart back out into the baggage-claim area with Enzo seated on its handle, face flat against Pietro's lapel like a dead doll, he locates the mother who loaned them the shorts. He hands them to her with a slight bow, clicking his heels in gratitude. She wears mustard-colored tights, a long red sweater and black boots, and tells him, in accented English, how good it is to see 'fathers really engaging with their children's basic needs'.

Mette Kaldstad said she'd meet him outside the baggage-claim area carrying a sign with his name on it. And there she is, plump, like a large hen, with that Scandinavian lack of feminine charm Italians enjoy ridiculing. To Pietro, she looks shorter than expected, nor does her coloring strike him as appropriately Nordic. Her eyebrows, he notices, are raised as if all life were a question she was afraid to answer wrong. In one hand she holds a stuffed penguin and a piece of torn cardboard with his name scratched onto it in ballpoint pen. The individual letters have been traced over and over, apparently to compensate for the thinness of the pen's line, and the 'iavo' of Dott. Pietro LoSchiavo is squeezed together into the last three centimeters because the earlier letters had been allowed to take up too much space – particularly those of his title. In her other hand, she holds a disposable camera. When she raises it to her eye, pointing at him, Pietro puts his free arm up to cover his face and wonders, suddenly, if this woman really is who and what she purports to be.

After the flash, their eyes meet. The woman nods, smiles broadly, and wiggles the sign, pointing to it like a grammar-school teacher saying, 'B is for Babbo,' her head bobbing. She gestures to the sleeping boy as if to say, 'Oh, how sweet,' then reaches out and strokes his sweat-dampened hair.

'Signora Kaldstad?' He straightens the leaning

child to place him more securely against his chest, offering her his free right hand to shake. 'I am afraid I must go immediately, though I hesitate to leave Enzo until he wakens. I presume Signora Nadarević told you about his incontinence? It ought to be checked again medically. There is a note about it in his pocket.'

'Don't you worry. We'll manage just fine.'

'Of course. And after all, he will be seeing his mother shortly. I understand that it is not as easy for her to cross borders as it is for you. Still, it must be difficult for her not to be here herself. Shall we phone her and let her know he is arrived safely?'

'No!'

Mette seems to him inordinately emphatic. 'I trust you will not feel offended,' Pietro states, 'if I ask you for some identification. After all, I am giving over a human life to someone I have never met.'

Mette rummages in her purse for a while and then extracts, triumphantly, the blue Croatian passport. She holds it open before his eyes, so close he has to crane his neck backwards to see it. 'It's Zheljka Nadarević's. Now, how would I have that if I weren't who I say I am?'

Pietro feels satisfied.

'I would wait but I have arranged for a return flight leaving in a very short time. My wife is alone, you understand. I ought, in fact, to proceed immediately to check-in. I really do apologize for handing him to you in this condition.'

'You don't have time to take just one picture of us?'

'I am so sorry.' There shall be no photo.

'Well. You go ahead now, Dottore LoSchiavo. And don't worry about the boy, he's in very good hands.'

Pietro hesitates. The moment of separation: Mette puts the penguin and camera in her purse and Pietro transfers to her grasp the handle of the luggage cart and the floppy body of his departing 'son', which she almost drops. After some fumbling, she gets his dead weight balanced, his face against her shoulder. The sleeping boy drools.

Then Dottore Pietro LoSchiavo leans down through the cool Scandinavian airport air to kiss Enzo goodbye. He tries one last time to waken him by shaking his face and patting his cheeks. 'Enzo? Listen to Babbo now . . .' The boy turns his head from side to side, nuzzling his nose across the nubby fabric of Mette's tan blazer and blinks as if about to awaken. 'Enzo. I have to leave you now.' The child does not wake up, but rather sinks even more deeply into open-mouthed oblivion.

Pietro looks at his watch, walks to the departures TV monitor, checks the flight number against the one on his ticket and shakes his head, as if in disappointment. 'I must go. I am terribly sorry, my flight, you see . . .'

Pietro pats Enzo's damp forehead. 'I really must go home to my wife. Give Signora Nadarević our regards.' He swallows. 'Enzo's papers are in his

184

carry-on bag, including the bishop's confirmation of his christening.'

He walks away, head erect, hands empty.

But then he turns, and comes back – to kiss the child goodbye. As his lips touch the boy's face, Pietro's nose registers not only Enzo's acrid and familiar smell, but also, inadvertently, the soapy, sweat-tinged odor of this woman whom he has never met but to whom he is relinquishing what was his only chance at parenthood.

He exhales sharply and walks away.

Maternal Instinct

Nothing like it ever was. Mette had Zero in her arms, his legs dangling, shoes banging against her knees, his kid-sweat salting their hair. Zero smelled like pee. His belly against her belly, his chest almost against hers, it was as if they were the same size, or even the same body. Yes, she thought, that's it – they were one body, as if no boundaries separated them, Siamese twins joined at the torso. Mette felt as if a pump had started up a brand-new heartbeat sending bright-colored feelings sloshing up and down inside her. She felt as if Zero had birthed *her*, as if this were the first time she'd ever had a body of her own and Zero had given it to her.

She tried the words out loud, right there among the rows of curved pink and blue airport seats with the loudspeaker announcing new arrivals. She whispered them over and over – 'A mother, a mother.' And then, 'My son, my son,' as if he'd been gone but now was back.

She felt she loved him right away. In fact, maybe she'd always loved him; ever since Zheljka first mentioned him he was already hers because Zheljka gave him away and Mette knew she could never do that.

Once Mette had Zero in her arms, a clarity came over her and she wasn't panicky any more about what the hell she was going to do with this kid because don't mothers simply know instinctively? She always did wonder though if a baby's mother could *really* tell the difference between a wet-diaper cry and a cold-breeze cry, or was that just fertile, phony women showing off? But she *could* feel a little of that in the airport, she felt sure of it, as if now she just *knew* what to do for him, as if she'd been handed the instruction manual along with the boy: Woman's Knowledge. Or maybe she'd always had it, right there in her belly, just waiting for the day they'd put him in her arms. *Just listen to me, will you,* Mette had to smile at herself, *saying they put him in my arms, like he was born and the nurses gave him to me! He gave him to me, Dottore, but of course he's not that kind of doctor.*

She could have stood there for ever, in an eternal moment of perfect union.

Nor was Mette scared any more about where to go. She had all the money she'd emptied from their account in her bag, and her car with a full tank. Of course she still didn't know what to tell Hans Olav. She'd prepared the guest room with the sheets with clowns on them that she'd picked up, and toys, which she'd hidden from Hans Olav in her dresser drawers. Everything at home was waiting, ready like one of those books where you turn the page and a house pops up, you pull the tab and a little kid waves.

Hans Olav, she was sure, didn't really mind not having children. It didn't leave a hole in his body like the one she felt get filled at the airport when suddenly she had Zero in her arms like a whole woman, not some cartoon lady any more with a big hole in her stomach you can see through to the flowered wallpaper behind her.

Not that her plans were less vague, but that she wasn't worried any more. She'd make everything all right for him because that's what mothers do – they make things all right for their kids. And wasn't she his mother now?

What language they would speak wasn't a problem either. It was obvious. Love. They'd speak the language of love.

Mette decided to phone Hans Olav. Then she thought, no, she ought to stay in Sweden and take the boy to the hospital, as Dottore had suggested. But it wasn't her thoughts that directed her feet, and Mette found herself at the phone booth calling Hans Olav at work, Zero balanced again on the handle of the luggage cart.

'I'm at a pay-phone in Sweden and I don't have much change. I'll tell you the number, and you call me right back.'

'Mette, are you joking?'

'Don't waste time. The number is 31 94 10 01. I don't remember Sweden's country code. Don't wait, it's important.' Hanging up, she missed the cradle the first two tries. When the pay-phone finally rang, she shifted Zero so he wouldn't suffocate against her lapel.

'What do you mean you're in Sweden? Why? Where in Sweden?'

'I don't want to tell you where I am because I'm not sure I'm coming home and I don't want you to be able to find me.' The strength of Mette's voice surprised her.

'Slow down, I don't understand a word. Where are you?'

'I said I'm not telling.' She smiled. 'If I tell you or not depends on what you say about what I've done.'

'Done? I'm supposed to be at a meeting in five minutes, I don't have time for games. You don't even sound like yourself.'

'What does myself usually sound like? I've never been so myself before . . . We've got a child, Hans Olav!' She was so happy.

'Whose child?'

'I'll only tell you if you promise in advance not to interfere, just to let me manage the whole thing. You promise?' Her voice quivered now.

But his sounded strict. 'You know perfectly well I cannot make promises about something the consequences of which I cannot guess.'

'Then I'm hanging up and you won't know where I am. Goodbye, Hans Olav.' She wasn't sure she'd really do it, but her husband seemed to believe she would.

'Wait! What I will agree to is not to take any action about whatever this business is until you and I discuss it. But only if you come home now. Agreed?'

'You always treat me like a child. I've never realized how much.'

'Mette. We can't have this argument by long-distance phone in the middle of a work day. Tell me what's going on and let's make some adult decisions about what to do.'

'I have Zheljka's son, Zero.' There it was.

'Did Zheljka ask you to get him?'

'Zheljka gave him up, Hans Olav. The man in Italy was going to send him to an orphanage so I took him instead. And I want us to adopt him.' It seemed to her such an obviously kind act that it disappointed her, hurt her, when Hans Olav's voice turned colder than she'd ever heard it. He even sounded sarcastic.

'And all this you have accomplished, I gather, without consulting either the mother of the child or your husband. You're unscrupulous!' Was his voice usually very warm? Now it froze her out, and she shivered, standing all alone, with a tiny, doped stranger drooling on her blazer.

'I'll come home.' She wondered if she might actually hate Hans Olav.

'I'll call Zheljka and Mesud.'

'No! If you do that, Hans Olav, I'm not coming!' Yes, she might hate him. 'I'll come home and we'll

191

talk first. Just you and me. Please, Hans Olav. Give this a chance.' He was silent for a minute. Mette heard the rustle of papers at the other end of the line and said a quiet prayer that he'd let her come home.

'That phone number, 31 and so on. The book says 31 is Göteborg. You're in no position to make demands, Mette. I could have the police after you before you turn around.'

Was he always this ready to get mean if she opposed him, which she never did?

'Tell me that you won't call Zheljka and I'll come straight home.'

'I won't call *her* until you're here and we've spoken. That much I'll agree to. But what can you be thinking?' His voice was warming again, though possibly because he was getting his way? 'You think we can have Zheljka's child in this small community without her finding out? Look, we'll talk later. It's a five-hour drive. I'll make up the guest room bed for the boy.'

'I did that already, before I left.'

'How long have you had this planned?'

There was so much *hurt* in Hans Olav's voice. Mette wished she were there and could put her arms around him.

'I'll be home as soon as I can,' Mette promised. And then added, 'I love you.'

'*Kristus*, Mette.'

They hung up.

*   *   *

It had grown dark and the Swedish–Norwegian border was still far off when Zero started moaning foreign words. Mette tried to give him the stuffed penguin she'd lifted at the airport but his hands lay limp. She asked, first in Norwegian, then in English, then in her best pidgin, high-school French: was he hungry? Was he thirsty? Did he have to go to the bathroom? When she said, '*Peepee?*' they understood each other for the first time. Mette turned off at the first roadside stop.

At that time of the evening, Mette and Zero were almost alone in the fluorescence of the clean pine cafeteria. Zero, still drowsy, made no protest when Mette took him into the ladies' room, nor when she took down his pants. It seemed to her that she knew just what to do and how to do it. *Maternal* was the word repeating in her mind's ear.

She washed his hands, gave the boy a big smile then gestured putting food into his mouth. Taking his hand, Mette walked Zero down the cafeteria line. All he pointed at was pink juice but she bought him a piece of banana cream pie too, and what looked like homemade *lefse* since the pancake was bumpy and the butter unevenly spread; Mette presumed Zero had never tasted *lefse*. He ate nearly nothing. When he only wanted to curl up on the itchy orange wool seat of the booth to sleep, Mette tried to pick him up, to carry him back to the car. But Zero wouldn't let her. So, hand in hand, they walked out. Mother and child.

No child's car seat, or even child-sized seatbelt,

had figured in Mette's plans, though that was mandated by law; she prayed she wouldn't get stopped at the border for having Zero strapped into the front seat next to her like a little adult.

She closed the car door on the passenger side, then got in behind the wheel. Mette turned to offer the boy a welcoming, maternal smile, but saw Zero's face contorted, bloodless, his eyebrows raised, mouth agape. He reminded Mette of Munch's painting of a scream, a silent scream.

'*Mama schena*, what's wrong?' Mette cried out to him, as if instinctively.

With his left hand the boy cradled his own right hand. Mette, it seemed, had pinched the boy's fingers in the car door. But he hadn't made a sound. So how could she have known?

II

FREE WILL

Sanitized

Even Hans Olav had to marvel at his capacity to compartmentalize, to do what must be done despite internal dissonance. Directly after the disturbing phone call from Mette, he successfully completed a complicated contract negotiation, and to the company's clear advantage; even as his wife, in God knew what state of agitation, wandered Sweden with her purloined human cargo, he took care of business. He compared his technique for concentrating selectively to how one listens to a concert on a short-wave radio: one scans the wavering signal and decides which sounds are music and which are static interference. His wife considered this capacity to be proof that he was a basically unfeeling person. No, he countered: he did feel – he felt with his thoughts.

About Mette for instance: she was a wounded soul when he married her and that quality remained part of the attraction. In the privacy of his mind, he compared how Mette never gave in to her despair to the way Wagnerian chords strive toward a zenith, however in vain. Mette would detest that analogy, of course, as she grumbled, 'Anti-Semite!' and slammed the living room door whenever he played Wagner.

But it was Mette's complexity which first drew him to her, as with Wagner. That, and her bravery. He thought the Norwegian word *tapper* described her, evoking the way H.C. Andersen's little tin soldier evinced a great courage in the face of some innocent, romanticized concept of danger and not of danger itself. Not that her courage was a pretense: it was quite real. Just that she kept herself from knowing how very real it was by first transforming it into a story of itself, like a fairy tale, and then boldly facing up to *that*. Hans Olav found this terribly attractive. Even sweet.

When he tried to imagine what it must have meant to grow up as she had, in the shadow of atrocities, Hans Olav grew furious on his wife's behalf. Though he never met her parents, he had seen the photographs and swore he could hear strains of doom in the atmosphere around them. Even in the photos of them as they aged, their faces resembled those of children shaken from a nightmare yet still in the grip of a monstrous netherworld more convincing than the domestic scene their waking eyes should have been freed to take in. And *those* were the only eyes little Mette had to look into!

Not that he blamed them; one doesn't ask the survivors of a Holocaust to let bygones be bygones. But when he pictured the child, Mette, gazing into all that horror, he couldn't help but draw a comparison to his looking into his own mother's eyes. One light summer evening he remembered in particular: it was before the war. He was only four, though large for his age, and the family had moved to their house on the fjord at Snarøen for the summer. While the maid put him to bed, his parents hosted a garden party on the terrace; through the open window, little Hans Olav heard grown-up laughter bobbing in a sea of dance music. And even with all her guests his mother still came in to kiss him goodnight carrying a bowl of fresh strawberries awash in sugary cream – just for him, though it was late and he ought to have been asleep. She leaned down to kiss him and the fragrance of her finest perfume blended with the essence of strawberries and the aroma of her sun-soaked skin. He remembered her creamy voice.

His mother was no longer alive. To him, the word *longing* meant first of all her, and first of all then. But what had Mette to long back to? he wondered. For her, there was no *before the war*. Longing, for Mette, must be like her bravery – something conjured up to compensate for what could never be. An invention. A necessary illusion.

How he loved his wife.

Besides the gentle shelter he knew he could provide for her, there was another lack Jewish Mette suffered which it lay in Hans Olav's power to compensate: position in society. Though the law was changed a century or so ago, Paragraph Two of the original Norwegian Constitution forbade Jews – and Jesuits – to enter the country. Who could say to what extent that still tainted the folk-soul of the land? Then there were the residual effects of the German occupation.

Not that his family took particular pleasure in his choice of spouse. Despite the fact that all of them – with the shameful exception of one quisling uncle – had supported the Resistance and prided themselves on being liberal, they still seemed to find the thought of having a Jewish relative somewhat disturbing. Hans Olav liked to remind them whenever they made some innuendo that, however expunged it might be from the public self-image, Norwegians had in fact contributed to the Final Solution. *Remember Uncle Ørnulf?* he'd say. *Remember November 26, 1943, the ship,* The Donau? He remembered; he was ten by the time enthusiastic Norwegians helped round up five hundred and thirty-two Jews to load onto a German ship for transport to concentration camps. Only twenty-five of them survived. Afterwards, Mette and her parents arrived as part of a small contingent of what Hans Olav dubbed The Replacement Jews, the eight-hundred-some-odd refugees to whom post-war Norway opened her borders in penance. 'It's our own damned fault she's here,' he reminded his more aggressive relations.

Once, early in his and Mette's marriage, he even sent a pointed quotation disguised as a Christmas card to one particularly condescending cousin; to, in fact, Uncle Ørnulf's son:

First, to set fire to their synagogues or schools and to bury and cover with dirt whatever will not burn, so that no man will ever again see a stone or cinder of them. This is to be done in honor of our Lord and of Christendom, so that God might see that we are Christians, and do not condone or knowingly tolerate [such] public lying, cursing blaspheming of His Son and of His Christians . . .

Second, I advise that their houses be razed and destroyed . . .

Third, I advise that all their prayer-books and Talmudic writings, in which [such] idolatry, lies, cursing and blasphemy are taught, be taken from them.

Fourth, I advise that their rabbis be forbidden to teach henceforth on pain of loss of life and limb . . .

Fifth, I advise that safe-conduct on the highways be abolished completely for the Jews . . .

In brief, dear princes and lords, those of you who have Jews under your rule – if my counsel does not please you, find better advice, so that you and we all can be rid of the unbearable, devilish burden of the Jews.

Martin Luther
On the Jews and Their Lies
Anno Domini 1543

He signed it, 'Family greetings from Mette and Hans Olav.'

*   *   *

Unlike his wife's family, his own people had lived
in one place forever. As he told Mette, his great-
grandfather built the Lutheran chapel the whole
neighborhood used – for their marriages, baptisms,
confirmations, funerals; generations of Kaldstads
owned a huge farm where the shopping center now
stood. They'd never been persecuted, never been
discriminated against, never been anyone's scape-
goat. On the contrary, it was *their* set who had
the ear of the king, *their* names on letterheads as the
leaders of bureaucracies, corporations, governmental
ministries, foundations; even the high-profile
activists, the powerful radicals, came from their
circle. And when they retired, their progeny took
over. His people, he admitted to Mette while they
were courting – and not without some pride – were
the closest thing the ostensibly classless, but
actually quite stratified, Norwegian society had to
an aristocracy. He could give her, the immigrant
Jew, membership in that, within certain limits. He
could give her Respectability.

And what could she give him? she'd asked.
'Care and comfort,' he'd answered, not telling the
whole truth: though he did not disdain his social
perquisites, he found the predictability of his set
unbearable. Those women with their thoroughly
studied, bourgeois sophistication. *Studied* sophistication, he had enjoyed reminding the women he
knew before Mette, because, unlike Denmark or
even Sweden, Norway's cosmopolitan history was

shallow; nearly all Norwegians were peasants, either farmers or fishermen, only a very few generations back. He found the women of his group, even the feminists among them, insufferably mannerly and correct. With them, there seemed no room for existential wind, for any of the *Sturm und Drang* of reality. Certainly, as he'd watched them all inbreed and then divorce they did seem miserable enough, but how banal.

Then along came Mette, who excited him to passions not befitting the standard rites of society's power brokers. Mette Stein, child of extermination, *tilintetgjørelse*, 'to-nothingness-making', with – though he never told her in just these words – that dearly deceptive, compliant surface, her eagerness, even desperation, to please, as if begging to be exploited. And with her marvelous undertone of confused and vengeful vulnerability, like a work of Shostakovich, a simultaneity of angst and pathos clanging painfully, filling its emptiness stabbingly the way a cube fills a hollow sphere.

Yes, he did feel with his thoughts, and the very thought of that counterpointed tension between Mette's appearance: contoured, cushioned, comforting; and her interior landscape: prickly, dark, excessive, tormented, even barren – just the thought of it made his heart wild.

Hans Olav had tried all these years to provide what he imagined as a *basso continuo*, against which her antitheses could collide: he would hold the dynamic tension in check, be the container for her chaos, though at times he had to reach out very far indeed to catch her, to bring her back toward harmony. And, for the last fifteen years, their system had worked.

Only, lately, something had gone awry.

It seemed to center on their inability to conceive. Some grief had indeed followed the realization that there would be no children, that he would beget no son to carry on the line. It mattered far less to him, however, than to his wife; childlessness seemed to panic Mette as if, looking in the mirror, she saw no reflection. Hans Olav assumed the approach of Mette's menopause would loosen her obsession's sway, but rather the opposite occurred: the less likely pregnancy became, adding age as yet another infertility factor, the more she seemed consumed with mothering, feeding, tending, caretaking. Not just her husband now, but whoever came into her sphere.

She invited home those unappealing refugees, for example. He had tried to like them, but couldn't help thinking they exuded into the atmosphere all the jangle of recently survived trauma but none of that single redeeming emanation he had perceived in the pictures of Mette's parents – humility. Why, he asserted, should one go out of one's way to show compassion toward victims who would blame even *you* for their troubles, though you had no role whatsoever in creating their war? Mette seemed to lack criteria for whom to take on, as if she wished the entire world to have emerged from her empty womb.

In fact, Hans Olav realized at his desk that afternoon after the phone call, as he organized the contract changes which his secretary would then key into the computer: it was ever since those refugees came to stay with them that Mette had been going wrong.

Now she'd gone off, and in secret, pinched part of some strangers' misery and mess, intending to adopt it into their lives. What did he want with a, most likely, disturbed child in his house? Just knowing the story of this Zero's conception was enough to put him off his feed. Should he want that horror in his face every day? It would be like having Mette's father as his son.

No. This time, Mette had clearly gone over some edge; it was so unlike her not to consult him. Yet there he sat, with a *fait accompli* in his lap, an already committed – well, if not crime, at least an immorality, a failure of ethics. Like a tale from some second-rate libretto.

The word *stueren* fit here, 'living room clean', house-broken, respectable enough to invite into your parlor. That's what Hans Olav had made of Mette.

And now look.

Repatriation

Twenty-five identical envelopes with an Immigration Office return address, twenty-five sweat producers guaranteed to flood fear into the veins of an already adrenaline-burned refugee group, had been meticulously lined up on the lip of the blackboard in the resale clothing store, in alphabetical order by last name. Zheljka stuffed the one with her name on it into her pocket. She'd deal with it later.

But then, the other women should begin arriving soon and Zheljka would be damned if she'd learn her fate second hand. So she opened what turned out to be a form letter from a certain Mrs Else Dagny Heyerdal Ruud.

Appointments regarding the repatriation of Bosnian refugees will begin on Tuesday, May 19, and proceed according to registration numbers.

Two days after May 17, Norway's national day, their annual glory-orgy of gratitude for chauvinistic yearnings gratified. A better date than most to start chucking the aliens out. *Repatriation*.

Newspeak, she called it. If Zheljka suffered from that disease called Nationalism, which she vowed she didn't, it certainly wouldn't be for Bosnia. Croatia, perhaps, or – yes, okay: Dubrovnik. Admittedly, Dubrovnik could rattle some shard of that bizarre and vicious ethnic fervor she'd watched transform the culturally sophisticated city of Sarajevo into a pit-bull arena, a city of jaws dripping blood.

Repatriated. Sent back where? Their old neighborhood? Had the war crimes tribunal in The Hague convicted her ass-rapist neighbor, Drago, the *Komandant* with his big dog? Or was he back on those same streets?

They finally had a reasonably good life here. Mesud had that job in the print shop, had recovered from his accident. And she'd even been considering finding herself a piano teacher, had been picturing the notes she used to play, imagining the penciled fingering notations on her old scores, the phrases marked *forte* here, *mezzopiano* there. She was coming back to herself, measure by measure.

Repatriation. All that effort to learn Norwegian, an ugly language spoken by a sum of people fewer than the inhabitants of a single Yugoslav province, and a small one at that – what use would that be back there? Sure, she knew her visa was only 'Temporary' but, as she had commented upon seeing that word stamped on her papers, what in hell isn't?

'Now that Bosnia is at peace . . .' Mrs Heyerdal Ruud's letter continued in another word-warp . . . *The war is over, you can go home now, Mrs Nadarević.* Now *there* was a song, like the triumphant march from *Aida* screeched off-key. *Home.* When she tried to imagine her mother greeting her, open-armed, in the raucous Dubrovnik sunlight the image boiled like a stuck frame of movie-film: the prematurely aged lady who would sit there, bolt upright with clasped hands on a rickety folding chair in their apartment's marble-tiled entryway, would be the very same cold bitch who'd refused to attend her own daughter's wedding, not because Mesud was a Bosnian Muslim instead of a Croatian Catholic, but because the 'primitive brute' only set the type for books instead of writing them. War isn't renowned for its salutary effect on already strained familial relations.

And Zheljka's father was still missing.

Go home?

What would Immigration do if she simply didn't show up for the appointment? Maybe she could get herself on *TV2 Helping You*, that exposé program, make one of those stinks they like to raise against incompetent, niggling little bureaucrats.

Or she could go underground, simply refuse to leave, the way that Albanian family had done, logging years in the cellar of a rural Norwegian church like kids playing hide-and-seek, clinging to base, safe as long they don't leave. Except the game – which happens to be their lives – can't go on.

And then there was Mesud. He was, and at this Zheljka snorted a laugh, *dying* to go 'home', to search for the bodies of his family, never mind that they were probably among the unidentifiables in one of those mass graves they'd been uncovering, a new bone-pile for every passing day. Most likely, his people had been killed, or rather murdered, or more accurately massacred, while the various forces of not only, but most especially, the Serbs were still doing piecework, still killing the *Balije*, as they liked to call the Muslims, with more passion than efficiency, one by one, by hand or boot or bayonet or rifle butt or machete.

But what about those relatives back *home*, those who, by some sloppy Serbian oversight, were left alive? How would they react to Mesud's sullied wife, that *Ustaša* whore who'd besmirched the Nadarević family name not just by getting herself gang-banged but by surviving? A story made the rounds of Sarajevo before the war about a teenage girl hailed as a martyr because she'd jumped to her death from a third-story window rather than let a bunch of boys 'dishonor' her family's name by raping her. It was Mesud's people themselves who'd designated her body the battleground, as if directing the Serbs' sights at her genitalia, whispering: *If you really want to humiliate us, that's our weakest spot. Just enter there and we'll believe you've won.*

Home.

*   *   *

But then again, Mesud's Norwegian stank. She couldn't figure out how anyone so musical could be so deaf to language. Maybe it was just Norwegian he refused to hear, those choppy, plodding words, all those weird vowels you have to warp your lips around so that you look the way opera singers do on TV when you turn the sound down on them.

No, it wasn't so easy to stay where they were either. But go back? Be sent back?

'They won't necessarily be returned to exactly where they came from,' she'd seen a safely groomed, thirty-ish female bureaucrat explain patiently to an invisible journalist, 'if that would involve territories which were reassigned during the peace negotiations.'

Ah! 'Reassigned.' Such a word acts as a canned lullaby for the makers of 'civilized' European policy. Who would think that even in a foreign language word-sins would clang and scrape? But they do.

Zheljka poured herself a cup of watery Norwegian coffee, longing for proper cappuccino, then decided to get out her passport and check if her registration number was written there. She presumed they'd be sent away on a first-in-first-out basis, according to some skewed idea of fairness, without asking who was fit to go, ready to go, *dying* to go.

She opened the raggedy patchwork purse and found her wallet. She kept her passport in the slot behind where she presumed others kept a picture of their kids. But it wasn't there.

Zheljka slid everything, notes, bills, receipts,

coins, from her wallet onto one of the school desk-tops, digging into every crevice, exhuming lint and shredded phone numbers, unable to believe the passport wasn't there somewhere. Then she heaped the contents of her entire purse onto the desk. When a torn tampon rolled off onto the floor she burst out crying. The tampon and such ready tears reminded Zheljka: she was pregnant. That ought to have been the first thing she'd thought of, not the last. What a mother.

Pregnant. And they would send her back to war, and call it peace. Norway might never feel like home to her, but at least her daughter – for that's how she pictured this baby, a girl she'd name Beate – could grow up feeling safe. Home in 'Ex-Yugoslavia' would always mean terror for Beate. She'd have a Croatian mother. She'd have a Muslim father. She'd have a cunt.

Loving Deceit

Hans Olav opened the heavy, mock old-fashioned, carved door and there they were, his wife and the boy, who, wrapped in a car blanket, resembled a heavy bundle of laundry. The music of his wife's emanation struck Hans Olav as new, atonal. And her eyes seemed to say, *Please*; to say, *To hell with you*; to say, *Jeg kan ingenting for det. Against this, I am defenseless.* He let them in, Mette and child.

The boy stirring against Mette's shoulder opened and closed his mouth, as if suckling. 'Let's put him right into bed,' Hans Olav whispered, then let them pass, climbing the stairs behind them rather than disturbing the sleeping boy by switching the arms which held him; if he walked behind his wife, were the weight of the child to destabilize her, he could break her fall.

Once up the stairs, however, Hans Olav passed quickly ahead of them into the same rooms where Zheljka and Mesud had stayed those many months ago. He turned on the reading lamp beside the bed to serve as a nightlight and, pulling back the bedcovers, exposed sheets he'd never seen before: on a background printed with juggling circus clowns, doves and balloons, a lion tamer repeated his feat of dominance, complete with whip, in diagonal bands across and down the bed. As Mette removed the boy's dungarees, a little pistol fell out which Hans Olav picked up and placed, carefully, beside the pillow.

'What happened to his finger?' he asked then, seeing the bulky gauze bandage.

'Shh,' Mette answered protectively, and went about threading Zero's limp limbs into the cowboy-and-Indian-patterned pajamas she'd located in one of his bags. Cooing softly, she tucked the boy's down comforter in around him and bent over to press her lips to his damp forehead. She looked down at his face for a long moment and then, as if reluctantly, left his bedside.

Hans Olav followed her. He didn't close the door to Zero's room – the guest room, he quickly corrected himself – but he did close the door to their own spacious and well-lit bedroom. It was 2 a.m. Mette might have expected Hans Olav to undress for bed, set his clock and go to sleep: she teased him often enough about being a creature of habit. But he didn't do that. He sat down on the bedroom rocking-chair and observed his wife preparing for bed, rubbing cream into the eczema sores on her arms, putting on her pink flannel nightgown and brushing her hair as if it were any other evening.

Except she made no eye contact with him, and spoke not a word.

'Well, Mette?'

'It's late. Why don't we talk tomorrow?'

'Major decisions are necessary tomorrow.'

'What major decisions? You said we wouldn't do anything.'

'Don't play dumb. The authorities have to be notified.'

Mette directed her response to the shoelaces she fumbled with, and spoke so softly that Hans Olav had to ask her to repeat herself.

'You can't make all the decisions,' he finally heard her say.

'I'll have to make them if you lose all perspective.'

'I've only just found *perspective*, Hans Olav,' came from underneath the bedcovers. 'I've never had such clear *perspective* in my whole life.' She seemed to address this assertion to the gold-braided lampshade near his face.

'What's clear is that you believe you can steal and get away with it.'

Mette's glance flew to her dresser.

'What you've done is stealing, Mette. Had you asked Zheljka's permission it would have been a different matter.'

'She doesn't deserve that.' For the first time since arriving back home, Mette looked at her husband directly; she even sat up in their bed to do it. 'She gave that child away! He was up for grabs. It was me or an orphanage and you may have a lower opinion of me than even I do, but I still think I'm better for that child than some institution.'

'That's not within your authority to determine.'

Mette threw the covers off and rose to her bare feet. 'But it's *yours* to decide? Right from wrong? You're so goddam righteous and holier-than-thou! Why have I put up with it all these years? I'm keeping this child, Hans Olav . . .'

'You make him sound like a puppy.'

'Even if I have to run away with him tomorrow while you're at work – since you'll go to work right on time come hell, or high water, or a new child in the house. What are you going to do about it? Keep me prisoner like a bird in a cage? Lock me up in some concentration camp, take away my son and gas me?'

Hans Olav sat blinking in his chair, letting her outburst vibrate the walls. He found a smile creeping onto his lips and tried to muscle it away; he wouldn't want her to think he was laughing at her. She was dear to him, this simple and extraordinarily complex woman – and that Holocaust note, waiting to be sounded in any dispute. Unrealistic as hell, yes. A bit paranoid, yes. But dear.

Mette flung open their bedroom door. 'If *our son* wakes or calls out, I, for one, want to be able to hear him,' she announced. Once back in bed, she turned her back on her husband, switched off the bedside lamp, nested down under the covers and said goodnight. A dim glow spread into their room from Zero's lamp down the hall.

216

Hans Olav, still dressed, rocked in the rocker, having decided to give Mette the last word. Instead of preparing for sleep he found himself, on an impulse, heading for the bedside of the sleeping Zero. The boy, having drawn his knees up tightly toward his chest, took up inhumanly little room so that the bed looked empty. Within Hans Olav, this child lying in his guest suite bedroom opened up an unnamed void, and, in seeming defiance of the comforting laws of physics, the boy managed to occupy that new empty space totally, yet without filling it at all. Zero, dark, small-boned and Slavic, looked not the least bit like Hans Olav. *And no child ever would.* Why, he wondered, did that disturb him more in this moment than it ever had before? His large palm felt drawn to touch the boy's sleep-flushed cheek. Hans Olav kept his hand there for some time, until his wrist grew stiff.

No. This was not his son.

And no. He would not tell Mette that he had already notified the authorities of the child's arrival in the country, nor tell her that they, in turn, had either called Zheljka or would do so first thing in the morning. And he would not mention the meeting he'd agreed to attend at the office of Else Dagny Heyerdal Ruud of the Immigration Services the following morning at 10 a.m. with the Nadarevićs.

Hans Olav reminded himself as he finally prepared for bed, after first spending an hour letting Mahler and Hennessy calm him down in the living room, that technically, though he had stretched the boundaries of veracity, he had not actually lied to his wife: on the phone, he'd only promised Mette not to call *Zheljka*. After all, he argued, when one negotiates with someone committing a desperate act, one stands outside the realm of ethics. One does whatever necessary, be that the making – or breaking – of expedient, even manipulative, promises.

Let Mette have this night's sleep, Hans Olav decided; she'd be faced with reality soon enough. Let her be the mother in her own home for this one night. Even if he could not be the father.

And so it was with tired and tender arms that Hans Olav embraced his wife when he finally got into bed that early morning, presuming her to be asleep. As he fitted his body behind hers, he felt her spine stiffen. Soon, though, Mette yielded. And then she wept softly, and whispered through her tears, 'Thank you, Hans Olav. Thank you for understanding.'

As he entered her then, slowly, from behind, she was still repeating it: 'Thank you, Hans Olav. Thank you.'

Fugue

Though the female bureaucrat phoning during Mesud and Zheljka's breakfast formed her words cautiously, her voice sounded intractable.

'Mrs Nadarević? Mrs Heyerdal Ruud from Immigration here. We know you've had your son brought into Norway illegally.' Zheljka's knees gave out; she dropped down onto the metal folding chair next to the telephone in their hallway. Son?

The voice kept at it: 'You refugees have been adequately informed that the Family Reuniting Policy applies only to those with *residency* visas – Bosnians get only *temporary* visas as you're to be repatriated. If you've broken the law, you may be liable for immediate deportation, if not criminal prosecution. And your son can't stay here, you know. Do you understand?' She paused. 'Mrs Nadarević? Are you there?'

Where? Was she where? After a pause, Zheljka let a sound escape which confirmed her presence on the phone line but was otherwise empty of meaning. As the message sank in, Zheljka felt herself split into

219

two: one Zheljka flew upward to hover by the ceiling, from which vantage point she hurled down caustic commentaries on the other Zheljka, the one still sitting, trembling, on the chair below. *And you thought you'd get away with it, bitch.*

'Son?'

'I've set up an appointment for you and your husband at ten o'clock this morning, here at the department. Mr Kaldstad will be here as well. It was misplaced kindness on their part to do this for you and I must warn you, Mrs Nadarević, failure to appear will escalate this into a police matter. None of us wants that, do we? By the way, this will take the place of your scheduled repatriation appointment, the one we sent you a letter about, so make sure you bring your papers with you. And your passport.'

'It is lost.'

'What is?'

'My passport.'

'Oh, Mrs Nadarević.' Mrs Heyerdal Ruud sighed as if the bureaucratic burden were a crushing one. 'Ten o'clock, please.'

'I'm not going to any meeting! There's no way the boy could be here.' Mesud chewed his bread and jam, as if nothing, nothing at all.

'And if he is?' she whispered, while the part of her hovering on the ceiling growled like a caged jackal, *That brute, dipping his bread in coffee, slurping it into his mouth. Victims of war, my ass. Child abandoners. Abusers. Criminals.*

Mesud swigged his orange juice, lit a Marlboro then took a long drag as if wishing this pregnant wife of his were exaggerating. 'Zero's not here, Zheljka. They just got their papers crossed. Or some anti-immigration fucker stole your passport and messed with your files.' He kept stirring sugar in his coffee, seeming to have lost track of how much was already there. 'Or maybe it's a Serb – they've got their agents here too, you know that. Nobody even knows about Zero here, we don't exactly go around bragging about him.'

Zheljka said something which he twice asked her to repeat – either because she spoke too softly or because he couldn't believe his ears.

'I told someone,' she said, the second time. 'I told Mette Kaldstad.'

Mesud's jaw dropped. 'That Jew lady, that jerk?'

The half of Zheljka still paralyzed in its chair saw nothing but Zero's face as he'd struggled against the short Italian man, and heard nothing but her son screaming *Mama!* as they dragged him off, as she let them drag him, screaming, inconsolable, furious, into the car that drove away with him. Why was he not dead? Why was she not dead?

Mesud pushed the table away from him so hard its metal legs scraped a gouge in the kitchen floor and then began to pace, tossing his head from side to side as if to dislodge undesirable images of his own, all the while cradling the arm he'd broken at the print shop as though it had not healed. His gaze fell everywhere and nowhere, but certainly not upon his wife.

Zheljka rose from her chair as if in a trance. At the front door of their apartment, she took her heavy navy-blue sweater from the hook and as that split-off, beastly commentator hovering above her howled curses at *that shit of a man who could make a woman give up her own child* Zheljka left and shut their apartment door behind her. She descended the single flight of stairs and exited onto the gravel parking lot that fronted the barracks-like refugee housing instead of a lawn. From there she turned right, gesticulating and muttering aloud like a mad-woman.

Where to go, to get away? She was freezing; though it was May, the cold hung on, as if winter were all there would be. Where she was headed, Zheljka had no idea. Maybe to the cemetery, to Beate. It was History she ran from and, to her, there was no stalker more tenacious, no trapper so cunning: its favorite victims are those who survive.

That was the moment that Zheljka's unborn son made his presence felt: for the first time but not the last, he kicked her.

Consecrated Ground

For the sadly attended Tuesday funeral of Signora Mariella LoSchiavo, a rarely used baroque Vatican chapel had been opened, proffered by Cardinal Fanfani, but on orders from above. Such *bontà* bespoke the debt of gratitude which the Holy See deemed it owed that esteemed bureaucrat, Dottore Pietro LoSchiavo, husband of the deceased. Not, of course, that anyone doubted that *il dottore* would have continued loyally and with cunning to expedite Church matters through capricious, even treacherous, governmental channels, even without this flattering encouragement.

The afternoon before the funeral, the briefest of obituaries had appeared in the most conservative newspaper, the one read both by Dottore's most respected colleagues and by his fellow Lodge members. This notice closed with a request, in seventeen-point italics, that, in lieu of flowers, donations be made in the good signora's name to the Santo Spirito Home for Children Orphaned by War.

Being unavailable to perform the rites himself, His

Eminence Fanfani passed the honor on to an obscure Father Angelo Angelotti. Fortunately, however, this pimply young cleric acquitted himself admirably. In his brief eulogy, evincing an exquisite tact, he skirted the equivocal circumstances surrounding Mariella LoSchiavo's demise, choosing to focus instead on her meritoriously constant, though forever unfulfilled, quest for motherhood. Father Angelotti was, of course, too solicitous – or perhaps too uninformed about the family's history – to enumerate just how many stillbirths the woman had endured with her maternal fervor yet unabated.

Besides the few actual mourners, the congregation seated before the boyish priest consisted of those matrons, clad perennially in black, whose faithful church attendance rescues clergymen the world over from the ignominy of casting their rituals useless upon empty furniture. A half-dozen such women sat scattered now among the pews, wiping their eyes, perhaps of the tears for some private or collective grief, perhaps of the discharge, often runny and yellowish, which tends to cloud the vision of the elderly. It was to this assemblage that the priest spoke fervently of Signora LoSchiavo's passion for parenthood. According to Angelotti, the deceased ought to serve as a model for all women, an exalted martyr in these days of diminishing family size and commitment.

The LoSchiavo family's physician and friend, Professore Benito Malluce, had canceled pressing appointments, including an operation on the hernia of a certain well-placed politician, in order to be by Dottore LoSchiavo's side. Any suspecting, or even any *knowing* observer, attempting to assess the state of mind of *il professore* would have detected in him not a twitch of either compunction or contrition. True, it was his unhesitating pen-stroke which had discreetly – and, he would add, compassionately – assured that Signora LoSchiavo's eternal soul might receive full ecclesiastical blessings. It was thanks to him that her earthly remains would be allowed to lie, for all eternity, within the cool bosom of the LoSchiavo family crypt, only two shelves to the left of her in-laws. Professore Malluce had often joked, though with that poker face of his one might easily have wondered if he was serious, that as far as he was concerned the two best inventions of mankind were anesthesia and lies.

Nor would the old family servant, Silvana, in service to the LoSchiavo family since Pietro was a boy, have appeared gripped in any struggle with the demons of conscience, neither as regards her complicity in keeping the emotionally unstable signora ignorant of Dottore's plan to un-adopt *that bedwetting little Slavic heathen*, Enzo, nor concerning the role she'd played in preparing to send the boy away while Signora LoSchiavo was off visiting her sister, Maria Grazia, in Perugia. Silvana appeared blithely unrepentant also for sneaking the three emptied sedative bottles out of the house hidden in her purse and then disposing of them in the garbage can behind her sister's moldy one-room flat across town where she spent her Tuesday nights off. All in all, she appeared to look forward to serving *il dottore* obediently for many years to come; yes, perhaps now even better than before, as she would suffer less interference.

There remained only one potentially contentious and marring presence in the echoingly empty and crumbling chapel: that self-same sibling, Perugian Maria Grazia. She sat throughout the service red-faced and puffing, as if inhaling not the fragrance of incense but the stench of sulfur. Her more noble hope – that her dear sister's name, and with it their family's reputation, be inscribed in honor rather than in infamy in the rolls at least of the Catholic Church, if not of the Lord God Himself – clashed within her against a seductive and compelling urge toward vengeance: that all the world might come to know on whose confessional list of very mortal sins her sister's suicide deserved to burn.

Beneath the peeling frescoes that cold spring morning, the hush of Mercy prevailed over the tumult of Justice. The ritual ended without incident. No reception was held afterwards.

Late that same night, after imbibing in quick succession several kitchen glassfuls of eighty per cent proof grappa, Pietro LoSchiavo stretched out on the narrow bed in the room he still referred to as Enzo's, abominably alone. On his back and with the lights out, he stared at the fluorescent stars he'd pasted on the ceiling with careful precision so that the boy might learn his constellations. But then spasms of weeping overwhelmed him, cramping his belly toward his chest, and Pietro could lie flat no longer; he had no choice but to roll reflexively onto his side and draw up his knees. His face cradled in cupped hands, the man rocked himself, crying out, again and again, 'Mariella, *cara mia!*' and, 'Enzo, *figlio mio!*' Until finally, exhausted, he yielded and let his sobbing take the sound of a single word – *zero*.

Nodding

No one asked the men if they wanted to meet up in some bureaucrat's non-smoking waiting room, the Lutheran business leader and the Muslim refugee, face to face on opposing couches. The one, after all, was in the country only at the grudging forbearance of the other. But there they, sat, each on his own green sofa – a popular color in a country which half the year lies buried in white – separated only by a low pine coffee table strewn with the cheery periodicals of the public sector's press. They nodded at first sight of each other, but did not speak.

Else Dagny Heyerdal Ruud came out to get them.

After expressing her displeasure at the absence of the wives, the bureaucrat showed the men down a bright corridor to her office, a white-walled room done up in what Norwegians call 'warm autumn colors', murky yellowed tones designed to bring out the glow in a blonde woman's cheeks. The decor failed, however, to brighten Mrs Heyerdal Ruud's prematurely aging visage.

While she was no relation to Thor Heyerdahl of

Kon Tiki fame, as evidenced by the missing 'h', Mrs Heyerdal Ruud claimed that the sharing of almost identical surnames had been the spark for her interest in things exotic, which then led to her career in Immigration. She was doing well, especially since her party, Kristelig Folkepartiet, had finally given in to the pressure and agreed to collaborate not just with the even more conservative Høyre but also with the most right-wing Fremskritts-partiet, though they were hardly *stuerene* much less Kristelige, with their hard-line, anti-immigration, racist rhetoric. But Kristelig Folkepartiet would do, and had done, just about anything to break the socialist Arbeiderpartiet's decades of control.

'This is a very serious matter,' she said, then seated herself on her like-new mustard-colored swivel chair and rolled up to her pine desk. 'Mr Kaldstad, I hope you realize you've been complicit in a crime. I can understand, Mr Nadarević, and I do sympathize, that you and your wife would want your son to join you here. Of course. And I know it must seem heartless of the authorities not to allow it . . .'

'We do not want him,' Mesud said.

Mrs Heyerdal Ruud threw a shocked glance at Hans Olav.

'It's too late to take that tack. You still must be held accountable for smuggling the boy into the country, and for involving Norwegian citizens in the scheme. I sincerely hope no fees exchanged hands; that would make the charges against you even more serious.'

Over Mesud's sputtered foreign sentences, Hans Olav interjected, 'You seem to have misunderstood the message I gave your department yesterday. It was my wife and I who took it upon ourselves to bring the boy here, to reunite him with his parents. The Nadarevićs knew nothing about it.'

'We do not want him!' Mesud snarled at Hans Olav. 'We did not ask you to do this thing. Why did you bring him here? Which *Četniks* ask you to do this?'

'Please don't shout, Mr Nadarević. What do you mean, you don't want him? Let me get this straight: *you* brought him here . . .' Her head turned first toward Hans Olav, and then, as if following the birdie in a badminton match, to Mesud. 'But *you* don't want him. Why don't you want him?'

'That is no business of you.'

Mrs Heyerdal Ruud's head began to nod up and down now, bobbing like one of those plastic heads attached by springs to a suction cup on the dashboard of a car, a car traversing bumpy terrain.

'Well, he can't remain here, regardless of who brought him – of who wants him and who doesn't. We've investigated your situation and you and your wife can safely return to Sarajevo. You're already scheduled to be repatriated this fall.' Mrs Heyerdal Ruud grew thoughtful; she swiveled her chair toward the window with its view of an identical brick government building across the walkway. Then, smoothing slowly and carefully each pleat of her khaki-and-cream-colored plaid skirt, she cogitated.

When she swiveled back to the men, Mrs Heyerdal Ruud looked quite satisfied. 'We can show some leniency here. I believe I'd be able to convince the Justice Department not to consider filing criminal charges against you and your wife, Mr Nadarević, and we'll simply move your repatriation date forward. You can just take custody of the boy and leave the country now, together, rather than wait until this autumn.' She offered another conspiratorial glance to Hans Olav as if to underline how tolerant and humane Kristelig Folkepartiet's Immigration officials were, not at all the impersonal and unfeeling agents the media so often made them out to be, especially since they took charge of the government.

Though Mesud's fists were clenched on his thighs, and though one of his feet moved much farther forward than the other as if preparing to flee, and despite the quickening of his breath, he appeared closer to weeping than to shouting. 'We do not bring him here! We do not bring him home. You take care of this, Kaldstad. You did it. You take care of it!'

'He is *your* son, is he not?' Mrs Heyerdal Ruud's intended rhetorical question evinced a surprisingly violent reaction. Mesud stood, turned, exited, and slammed the door behind him, all in a single movement.

In the ensuing silence, Mrs Heyerdal Ruud propped her head in her hands, elbows on the desk, rubbed her eyes for a moment and then sighed. 'You see what you have done? You're a person with a

232

position in society and you should know better. Your misplaced kindness will end up hurting that family very badly.'

Both the Heyerdals and the Ruuds belonged to Hans Olav's set; this woman might not know it, but he'd gone to school with her husband, Christian Ruud, had even dated the man's sister, Liv, albeit briefly. He decided to negotiate openly with Else Dagny. 'I didn't want Mr Nadarević to know this – if he intends vengeance, let it be directed against me – but it was my wife who brought the boy in, without my knowledge, without anyone's knowledge. We're childless. She refers to what she has done as "rescuing" the boy.'

'In my job you learn that it isn't so easy to decide whom to rescue.'

'My wife's parents were Hungarian Auschwitz Jews and she's been quite upset since these refugees stayed with us. So I hope we'll be able to work this out without legal complications. And, of course, without publicity.'

'The State is going to have to take over caring for the child until this gets worked out legally, you understand. And you know, too, that you and your wife can't keep him: adoptions have to follow strict procedures.' She swiveled to reach the telephone on the table behind her. 'Look, I'll get someone from Child Protective Services to go with you and pick up the boy until we can sort this out, but I don't think you have to worry after that. He's our responsibility, not yours.' Instead of making a call herself, however, she handed the phone to Hans Olav. 'Why don't you call your wife now and have her get the child ready?'

'It's too risky. She'll probably take the boy and bolt.'

'Immigrants. Everything was much simpler before they came. Don't you agree?'

When No One Screams

My chest will crush me with all of these pictures, and I'll die – no, it's too late for that – missed my chance when their Četnik fists smashed my face against the floor. I could have tried running, there was that moment, yes, I was on the floor under his boot, his knife against my throat, gravel on my tongue, that moment I quit struggling: *Shut up, Nadarević, or die. You decide*! I shut up, I did nothing. When they released me as a prisoner did I go back to my division in Sarajevo? No. I went west to Split, to be a refugee. To do nothing; what a coward. I do nothing.

Like when the snipers on top of one of the burned-out boxy apartment blocks, or maybe up on the hills, like on Mount Igman, when some sniper decides the day is a fine one, I might be on my way to anywhere, maybe bringing my mother and Senada firewood, like wood from the train station benches we'd bashed off their bases. Or maybe I'm getting off one of the trams that still limp along. Could be anytime and then, pop! And somebody is down.

Screaming in pain, or lying flat and frayed, his chest tufted like the torn-up mattress we put in front of the glass door to the balcony of my mother's fourteenth-floor, broken-elevator apartment to deflect bullets, though who are we kidding, it doesn't stop them. And what do we do when he's lying there, mattress-floppy and bleeding? We're all running for cover, covering our ears, falling over one another, fighting for a place at the bottom of the heap.

And then waiting. Is this a siege? A barrage? Or has some Karadzić psychopath dedicated a bullet to just that one guy, the one that's hit, the one wearing the suit? Who would put on a suit during a war? But this guy had a suit on, and a tie, he even looked reasonably neat, till the bullet shredded his shirt.

Then what do I do, when it seems like the bullet wasn't for general sport, was meant for him alone and not for me? Or maybe it *was* meant for me but that poor asshole got it by mistake. What do I do? Should I stop and check if he's breathing? How could I? What if I stopped for every corpse? What if every time somebody died everybody stopped, even for a second? Stop now. And now. And stop three times now.

No, I keep on going.

Except for that kid, because he was screaming. Yes, one was a kid, screaming, and he was little, I couldn't do it, just run past him. I tried. I made it almost all the way around the building but then I turned around, I got low to the ground, a dumb idea

236

when the sniper is high up, on Igman or up on one of the apartments – I'd have been a smaller target standing up than creeping on my belly like a cock- roach, crawling on my stupid belly and dragging the screaming little bastard by his feet along the pave- ment when I could have just picked him up. No, I dragged him so his ski jacket and his shirt bunched up in his armpits, scraping naked skin along the concrete, or was it cobblestone, or tarmac? I can't remember.

But when it was a grown-up who was hit, even a woman, and when the grown-up wasn't screaming, who knows if he was dead, or she, maybe only just unconscious, but anyhow not screaming, then I didn't stop. I didn't. And now I don't even help a kid. Zheljka's kid.

And I still keep dreaming at night that it's me there, lying shot on the city pavement and I'm trying hard to scream, and I can't make any noise, and there's all these people around me. It's me lying on the pavement in this dream, I've fallen against the curb at the tram stop and some guy with a pair of pliers is standing over me and I think he's going to hit me and I've already been shot, I'm bleeding. I can't move a muscle, nothing, not an arm, a hand, I've got nothing to protect me from this fucker with the pliers, and I've already been shot and I can't even scream. But that guy doesn't hit me. In this dream I keep on having, he doesn't hit me. I'm lying on my back, the sky is a lovely blue, and everything looks familiar, like it was before the war, before we cut down all the trees, before the buildings all got bombed out. And this bastard with the pliers is standing over me and I'm shot but I'm not screaming and what he does is this: *He treats me like I'm in his way*, like he's really in a fucking hurry to get some place and the bloody carcass of me is in his way. And with the hand without the pliers he holds onto the tram-stop railing and for a moment he straddles across me. For a moment I see him over me, his gray-trousered crotch up there in the blue Sarajevo sky, framed by those beautiful buildings.

And then he just saunters off. People on the tram look the other way, ladies with their shopping bags, like nothing, like nothing at all.

Flight

Mette had been rushing about all morning, preparing to leave. When she'd awakened and thought back on her conversation with Hans Olav the night before, she had realized it would never work. Something in Hans Olav's manner, too, as he leaned over to kiss her goodbye had confirmed her worst fears.

She ran upstairs to her dresser, now, two steps at a time to grab a fistful of underwear, then downstairs to the kitchen to stuff more food into one of Zero's duffel bags. She zipped it and dragged it to the front door next to his other bag.

I know Hans Olav, Zero, she half-whispered, *and he's not going to let me keep you. He cares more about rules than about me, and about you he doesn't care at all. Somehow or other, he's going to take you away from me, even if it means you end up in some orphanage, in Sarajevo or God knows where.*

Mette had already dressed Zero, in the clothes he'd arrived in the night before. He sat, now, on the floor of the guest suite sitting room fiddling with some tin soldiers Mette had taken for him, seeing how far their legs would bend and their bayonets twist before they broke.

I have to rescue you, get you out of this country-hell, out of Western Europe altogether. I've got the car, and all that money I took out before I went to Sweden to get you from Dottore . . .

All the money, Mette realized while making sandwiches, was still in her dresser. She flew back upstairs, stopping briefly at the landing to catch her breath.

I'll take care of you, Zero. You can trust me.

In the bedroom, Mette perched, wobbling, on the rocking-chair she'd dragged over to Hans Olav's wardrobe to reach the suitcase he kept there. Then from the top drawer of her own mahogany dresser Mette grabbed the wad of money. From the third drawer, she dug out of hiding the violet velvet shawl containing Zheljka's passport, Dottore's letter and the resale-store coins, all seventeen of them. She placed the whole bundle, unopened, straight into the suitcase.

We could go to Sweden first. It's easy to cross the border. And then . . . Well, then . . .

Mette stood now in her white marble bathroom, her hands filled with toiletries, cocking her head first to the right, then to the left, holding her breath as she tried to imagine where they could run to.

We could go to Hungary! I've never been to Hungary. Where my parents are from. I don't think we'd need visas. And even if we did, people pay bribes to get into Western Europe – buying our way out ought to be cheap. Everybody, the Slavs and the Pakistanis, the Arabs – everybody's heading this way, not the other way. It would be easy!

Mette shoved her traveling cosmetic kit into the suitcase. And some clothes. And the camera.

When we get there, to Hungary I mean, we could go to my parents' village. I lied to Zheljka about them being from Budapest and the university, they were just peasants, from a little place called Lonya. There must be somebody who knew my parents before the war, even after all these years. They can't have killed every Jew in Lonya, can they? Besides, Jews are moving back to Eastern Europe and opening up the old synagogues, I saw it on television, there's a big new one in Lithuania or someplace. Well, maybe not big. But being Jewish is like a club – they have to take me in. And you'd be with me.

It'll be sort of like going home, for both of us.

Mette sat all her weight on the overfilled suitcase, hoping it would close.

I've almost got all the stuff together. Your bags are still packed, I haven't had time to unpack them. And I've got food, Jarlsberg and tubes of caviar. And lefse. *I know you'll love* lefse, *Zero.*

Mette lugged her suitcase down the stairs. Standing with the luggage before the big front door, Mette heard herself proclaim, aloud, 'We'll have such a good life!'

The Door

Just as she finishes stuffing the very last thing into Zero's nylon duffel bag, the penguin from the airport that she'd dress in the baby sweater she had knitted, Mette thinks she hears someone at the front door. She runs to the upstairs hall window from where she can check who's there without being seen. If it's Hans Olav she'll have to grab the boy and the bags and make a run for it through the carport door, putting the car in neutral then letting it roll down the driveway silently.

Hans Olav would have been bad enough; knocking on her front door is Zheljka.

Mette gets hold of Zero and drags him into 'his' bedroom to hide, putting her finger to her lips in hopes that the signal for 'be quiet' is international. He screams anyway, twists his wrist from her grip, and, his back to the wall, aims his cap gun at Mette's head.

'I hear him, I know you've got him!' Zheljka shouts from outside the door, her knocking becomes a pounding of palms, knuckles, fists, demanding entry as if she'd never wanted anything in her life except to be with her son.

Mette opens the big front door, to shout into Zheljka's face, 'He isn't yours any more! You gave him up!'

Zheljka pushes her aside, wild-eyed, following the sounds of Zero's screams, taking the stairs two at a time. But when she gets to the open guest room door, Zheljka stops. She sees Zero, but she just stands there, looking at' him – her Zero, slightly taller than before, but still skinny, still crying, still armed with that same toy gun.

Zero doesn't scream now, doesn't even breathe for the moment it takes him to register who is there, who he is seeing. Then, he acts as if no time had passed. He runs to his mother with outstretched arms, crying, over and over, 'Mama!' at exactly the same pitch and volume, and with the very same desperation as he had cried it during their last moments together, as the Italians were taking him from her. Gun in hand, he hurls himself around her bony hips. Her arms fly up into the air, her eyes and mouth shut tight.

Zheljka's hands, as if in some slow-motion life of their own, then reach down under Zero's arms to lift him into an embrace. He winds his legs around her waist, locks his feet together at the ankles, locks his arms tightly around her neck, buries his face into the folds of her throat, and sobs. Zheljka burrows her face too into her boy's flesh. But as she breathes him in, kissing him, and weeping, Zero unlatches

244

his ankles and with his free right foot starts to pat Zheljka's body rhythmically, his right heel hitting her harder, faster, and soon he is kicking his mother – violently, woundingly – even as he kisses her, as he hugs her, hard.

Mette watches the two of them for a moment, listens to them cry. Then she walks, slowly, to her bedroom, curls up on the bed, knees to chest, and with her arms covers both her eyes and ears.

This is the household to which Hans Olav arrives, along with a uniformed policewoman – just a girl, really – and a long-haired fellow from Child Protective Services. Words failing them, the men resort to force. They yank open the mother's arms and then, to pry the boy loose, have to brave his punches, kicks, bites, threats, pleas until finally they have wrested him from the embrace.

The well-trained policewoman manages to get the struggling Zheljka pinned so she can't run after Zero. A captive in the Norwegian mock old-fashioned Kaldstad doorway, Zheljka watches, yet again, Zero's tiny body be taken away.

When he has the child strapped into the car, the Child Protective man slams and locks all the doors and then drives off.

Zero is still screaming.

Epilogue

The Unnamed Refugees on the
Seven o'Clock News

Zheljka is in her own bed, knocked out from weeping about the boy and from the sedative Hans Olav's doctor injected her with to stop her hysterics. Mesud comes in carrying a plastic bag containing his shaving equipment, toothbrush, comb. He draws the curtains against the Nordic evening sun, listens for Zheljka's slowed breathing, then reaches under the bed to pull out his nylon zipper bag. Quickly, quietly, he fills it with his belongings.

Before leaving the room, Mesud leans down through the semi-darkness to stroke his wife's damp forehead. He knows now that his enemies have won, that it is *their* womb his baby is growing in. There is a limit to what a man can forgive.

Mesud kisses his wife softly on the forehead. 'You can keep their son, my Zheljka,' he whispers. Then he kisses her hard, on the lips. Zheljka stirs only slightly and Mesud, bag in hand, closes the door as gently as he can.

In the hallway, not even taking the time to light a

cigarette, Mesud sits on the metal folding chair next to the telephone to look in the phone book for the number of the television news desk at TV2.

The switchboard operator has to ask him to please, speak up. She needs him to repeat himself three times before she finally deciphers his heavily accented request to talk to whomever is in charge of *TV2 Helping You*, the program that goes to bat for people when all else fails, the one whose aid Zheljka had planned to enlist if the government insisted she, as they called it, *repatriate*.

Mesud tells the program director that he fears the five-year-old son of a lady seeking permanent asylum in Norway – a pregnant lady – is about to be sent back to Bosnia without his mother. He doesn't tell the man this lady is his wife. He supplies Zheljka's, Zero's and Mrs Heyerdal Ruud's names, but refuses to give his own. When the man presses for details, Mesud hangs up.

Taking his jacket from the hook and picking up his bag, Mesud locks their door. Then he slides his key under it. Descending the stairs, he exits the front door, crosses the gravel parking lot and is gone.

Once the program director plucked the meaning of Mesud's story from the mix of mispronounced Norwegian words, he knew he had a plum to pass along to his buddy in the newsroom – a real human-interest scoop in these times of hot debate over which foreigners should, as one right-wing extremist from Fremskrittspartiet put it, 'be permitted to sully

Norway's cultural homogeneity in the name of tolerance'.

His friend in the newsroom loved it. As did the folks at NRK – radio *and* TV – as well as TV Norge and all the newspapers, especially the tabloids. The story sold even better as the delicate fingers of investigative journalists exposed its more piquant elements: the smuggling in of an illegal alien, or maybe it had been a kidnapping. The mass rapes.

Of course, the reporters, who were just doing their job after all, did get stonewalled here and there. Those trying to interview Hans Olav Kaldstad, for example, got nowhere, though they did have other sources. Just who were these sources, Hans Olav wondered. How the hell had they learned that the government was threatening legal action over what they were calling 'the barren woman's bizarre behavior involving a Bosnian boy'? Who told them to inquire if Mette weren't actually Hungarian – and Jewish – and not Norwegian at all? And where the devil had the rumor started that he and his wife had once thrown the refugee couple out onto the street? Such leaks and disinformation, Hans Olav figured, must be coming from someone on Mrs Heyerdal Ruud's staff.

Having camera crews at the door put the Kaldstad family's reputation in jeopardy: the self-imposed restraints on the Norwegian press, which nearly always stopped them from divulging the identities of those facing possible prosecution, did nothing to prevent the neighbors from figuring it all out. Hans Olav grew even more determined in his reticence.

He also forbade Mette to answer either the doorbell or the phone. Not that she wanted to, of course. She had something far more important to tend to than officials out to characterize as crimes her bold acts of charity – a pure-bred springer spaniel, barely twelve weeks old, which Hans Olav had brought bounding into their lives on clumsy puppy paws, yapping, drooling, scratching, having 'accidents', shredding newspapers, then taking a nap, warm and sweet-smelling all cuddled up on Mette's lap. Mette named him 'Shlomo', Hebrew for Solomon, ostensibly after her father's father, but, actually, in honor of the wisest of kings, the one who knew that to save a child a truly loving woman could even give him up.

As the media focus heightened, the public's response weighed in on the side of granting the refugee woman and her child permanent asylum. To this challenge to her department's decision-making authority, Mrs Heyerdal Ruud objected strenuously: 'We mustn't permit sympathetic opinion polls, incited by sensationalizing journalists, to determine Immigration policy.'

To which Mohammed Tajih of the organization for immigrants' rights countered that, apparently, without the pressure of the media, public policy risked abandoning all pretense of compassion. What would have become of the Holocaust Jews if no one

252

had taken them in? Did the government intend to renege on the long-standing Norwegian tradition of solidarity with those disenfranchised or oppressed?

After ten days, during which time the story progressed from *Dagbladet's* tabloid-sized page fourteen to page six to page three, the Minister of Justice herself finally spoke to reporters on the topic. Obviously, she could not comment on the merits of the specific case; it was her sworn duty 'to await the results of the re-evaluation being undertaken by the committee whose mandate it is to re-evaluate such things'.

'However,' she said, 'I do agree that while the investigation is taking place the boy ought certainly to be returned to his mother.'

The reunion is being played out, complete with lights, cameras and microphones, on the gravel parking lot in front of Mesud and Zheljka's apartment building in the chilly May wind. Mesud, of course, is not there.

With passers-by gaping, a gang of male journalists and photographers, carrying both still and video cameras, takes aim. A policewoman emerges from an olive-green government Volvo holding in one hand a nylon duffel bag and in the other the hand of a dour, skinny boy. He is dressed in what appears to be brand-new clothes – an ice-blue windbreaker, jeans, Adidas sneakers – although everything seems one size too large.

The focus is on Zero as he searches the crowd to find his mother, even if, there being some things in

Norway the press still can't get away with, the TV stations' editors might be expected to protect the refugees' privacy by blurring their faces when broadcasting the piece. Blurred or not, there's no scoop to be had: the boy's vacant expression barely changes when he and his bag are brought to his mother, nor when his hand is transferred from the policewoman's to hers. When Zheljka leans over as if intending to pick the boy up, all the cameras zoom in tight, hoping, perhaps, for tears. But Zheljka doesn't pick him up. Only his duffel bag.

Zero stands, then, with his face close to, but not touching, his mother's midriff, arms at his sides, his head behind the bouquet of microphones. A camera moves in tight on the toy pistol with the taped white handle the boy holds in his hand as a TV interpreter squats down before him.

'How does it feel to be coming back to your mother?' he asks, speaking Serbo-Croatian with that sing-song breathiness kindergarten teachers-in-training use to address small children. Then the man accidentally knocks his microphone against Zero's mouth, hard. The boy winces, jerks his head away, squeezing his lips together and closing his eyes tightly as if squelching tears.

'How do you feel about having your son back?' the interpreter is demanding of Zheljka while pushing his microphone up through the crowd of mikes and in toward her mouth so that the swarming cameramen all raise their equipment at the very same moment, abandoning the boy and latching their gaze onto his mother instead, who stands bolt upright, pinned by the media crush into the doorway of the block of refugee flats. They are all over her through their viewfinders, one cameraman panning, very slowly, down her pregnant belly, another closing in, his knife-sharp focus probing her face, her lips, as reporters poke their questions at her louder and faster, until they are pounding her with questions, all of them at once:

'What will you do if they won't give you asylum?'

'Did you pay that woman to get your son back for you or did she kidnap him for herself?'

and, 'Why isn't your husband here with you today?'

While in the undercurrents of the air around them shriek the unasked and unaskable questions, the lewd or only wicked, interesting questions:

You tried to get rid of the boy once already – are you so sure you want him now?

and, *Is it true your husband left you because of the kid?*

and, especially, *What is it like to be gang-raped?*

Zheljka flees into the building and up the stairs with her son running after her. She locks and bolts the apartment door, then leans her weight against it.

Zheljka, her womb a clenched fist, looks at Zero. Zero, hand jammed in his pocket, clutches his gun.

THE END